# TAKE THE PATH

Anthology of Award-winning Short Stories

ISBN-13: 978-0-9851833-1-8
ISBN-10: 0-9851833-1-4

# DEDICATION

This anthology is dedicated to those who know what path to take

To the authors featured in this book: Scribes Valley thanks you for your time, patience, trust, and talent.

.

# CONTENTS

# TAKE THE PATH
## A Foreword by David L. Repsher, editor

Anymore, it seems the world is on a fast track, a wide and hectically flowing track. Everyone is rushing toward something, but many times we have no idea what that something is. We want to get where we're going *now* not later. Time is at a premium, but we want it in increasingly smaller increments: seconds not minutes. We want our communications, our information, our very lives to happen ASAP.

No longer can we wait to talk face to face with friends and loved ones. We grab some electronic device and whip off a message, then decry the time it takes for them to respond. Microwave ovens, once the epitome of speed and efficiency, have become objects of ire as we pound on them, berating them for taking *seconds* to warm our food. Libraries, places we once scheduled time to visit, to walk the aisles, to run our hands over the rows of books and *smell* them, are now at our fingertips; books downloadable as mere impersonal files we never touch.

Where are the quiet times? The times when we looked forward to being with family and friends, face to face, eye to eye, actually enjoying the time we spend together? The times when we put our feet up and open an actual book with pages that we have to—heaven forbid—turn?

Those times can be yours again. All you have to do is jump out of the fast lane, get off the broad and rushing highway, leave the electronic devices in another room, pick up a book, and simply TAKE THE PATH.

# FIRST PLACE

## WEDNESDAY NIGHT GIRL
©2013 by Ronna L. Edelstein

The water nibbles at her toes and swallows her feet, legs, and thighs. Still not satiated, it gobbles her stomach and chest, arms and neck. Only her head remains free from the water's ravenous appetite. The water waits patiently, allowing Vera to decide whether she will deprive it of dessert by wading back to the shallow end of the pool or whether she will give it a final course by walking further into the deep end and letting it completely devour her.

Vera stands still, uncertain about what to do. She stares at the water, hoping to discover some sign—perhaps an image of her children or parents—that will lead her to choose life, but all she sees is the uncaring and unforgiving water. She contemplates turning around to give Doug one more chance to make amends— one more chance to pretend that he had not agreed to a Saturday afternoon at the pool with Vera, all the time knowing he would not extend the afternoon into an official Saturday night date. She will give Doug one more chance to blow her a kiss; if he does, despite her hurt, she will reach one arm out of her almost watery grave to grab the kiss and gently place it upon her lips.

But Vera knows that no kiss awaits her. In the silence of the backyard pool, she hears Doug gathering his legal files; when he thumbs through the pile to make sure everything is there, the papers whimper like the final flutter of the wings of dying birds. Vera hears Doug close his briefcase—the clamp snaps as if a squirrel were biting into an acorn. Then, the gate—the one her friends, the vacationing owners of the pool, never remember to oil—squeaks. Doug has left, leaving Vera alone in the water.

Vera again searches the water, silently willing Doug's reflection to appear but, unlike Vera, the water seems to understand that Doug is not special enough to hold onto. Doug is neither tall nor handsome. When with him, five-foot-eight-inch Vera has to wear her flattest flat shoes and further hunch her already round shoulders to appear shorter. Doug's thick black beard masks him in darkness, like a villain in the silent movies Vera learned about from Grandma. His teeth, as white as the chalk Vera uses on the blackboard in her classroom, gleam against his swarthy complexion, creating more of a smirk than a smile. Although Doug's appearance unsettles Vera, like a dinner that does not agree with her or a play that haunts her long after the theatre has gone dark, she has spent the past four months in an adulterous relationship with Doug.

Left hollow by a disastrous marriage, scarred by a wallflower adolescence, and destroyed by a lifetime of jarring maternal judgments, Vera needs to find beauty and goodness beyond Doug's unappealing façade; she needs Doug as if he were the life jacket drifting near the diving board. The fact that Doug wants to have sex with her—the phrase "make love" would distort the nature of this unloving friendship...tryst...relationship? —gives Vera a deluded sense of worth and self-esteem. She, the cockeyed pessimist, and he, the cocky controller, make an odd twosome, but all Vera cares about is being appreciated, even if the appreciation lasts for only brief gasping moments in bed.

A cloud floats across the sun, causing Vera to shiver in the momentary chill. The sudden coolness also reminds Vera that she cannot remain forever in the middle of the pool—too far from either the murky deep end or from the set of silver steps in the distant shallow end. One more minute, Vera thinks, just one more minute before deciding whether to move forward to a watery death or move backward to a quicksand life outside the pool.

Her best friends, the physician and his wife who live in the house with the pool, had warned her this would happen. "Doug is a player," the doctor had said. "Doug will use you and abuse you," his wife had added. Neither had mentioned the moral implications—that Doug was divorced, but that Vera was technically still married (as Vera stands in the water, she wonders whether being technically still married is like being a little bit pregnant) since the judge had not yet pounded his gavel and emancipated her. Vera contemplates foregoing drowning for the usual death by stoning reserved for adulterers. She pictures all of Doug's past, present, and future lovers circling her, mocking her for her stupidity for falling in lust—love? —with such a Lothario, and hurling stones—large and small, round and sharp—at her breasts and belly and thighs—all the places Doug once caressed and kissed.

And Vera knows for certain that Doug has had—and will continue to have—past, present, and future lovers. One Wednesday night, just as she and Doug were about to enter his bedroom, Doug had received a call from his office. "I have to go back to the office to pick up a file," he said.

"No problem," Vera replied.

"Wait for me," he ordered.

"Sure," Vera acquiesced.

The minute Vera had heard the roar of Doug's red sports car and seen the glow of the headlights through the living room window, she had gone to Doug's study, sat in Doug's black leather (the same black leather of his car's seats) swivel chair, and picked up his datebook—also bound in black leather. She needed to assure herself that Doug, like her, stayed home on Saturday nights to wallow in *Lawrence Welk* reruns, and that he did not go out with other girls he deemed more suitable for the traditional date night. She needed to determine whether Doug would forever see her only as a Wednesday night girl.

Her sin of adultery had made reading Doug's private datebook seem like a misdemeanor. Without hesitation, then, Vera had opened the book. While she found her name penciled in for the next few Wednesdays, the upcoming Saturday night page contained only one word: Barbara. Not Babs or Barbie or Barbra without the *a*, but Barbara, the perfect name for a society lady or executive. Vera had said the name aloud, enunciating each "Barbar-a" syllable as if spitting wads of phlegm from her throat. She wondered where Doug and Barbara would spend their Saturday night. Would Barbara have to pay for her movie ticket, or did Doug's Dutch Treat rule only apply to Vera? Would Barbara spend the night in Doug's bed, or would her Saturday night status end at the stroke of midnight?

One glance at the next week told Vera that Doug had replaced Barbara with Marci as his Saturday night girl. Vera's daughter had a Barbie doll she named Marcy with a *y*, not an *i*. The *i* seemed pretentious, as if this Marci were trying to stand out from the Marcy crowd. Doug, who had always refused to dance with Vera, even in the seclusion of his living room, would probably take Marci to a club where he and she would sip red wine, stare into each other's eyes, and sway together to the music. Marci may make it to Sunday morning, but she would not make it to the next Saturday week: Doug had penned in the name Deb.

As the water continues to wrinkle Vera's skin, making her look as old and tired as she now feels, Vera ponders the obvious question: Once she had "met" Barbara, Marci, and Deb, why had she waited for Doug to return? She could have grabbed her car keys, slammed shut the front door of Doug's townhouse until the stained glass decorative pane shattered, and then driven home. But Vera had felt homeless—stuck in a marital house with the estranged husband she hated, the children who reminded her of her mothering flaws, and the woman—herself—who filled her with loneliness and disdain. That Wednesday night, and for many Wednesday nights to come, Vera prostituted herself in a futile attempt to feel less alone. She succeeded only in making herself more miserable and lonely.

With her right hand, she creates circles in the pool's water; one circle leads to another and another and another, just like one decision—her decision to meet Doug at a darkened movie theatre on an unusually frigid spring day four months earlier—had led to more dalliances and deceptions and disappointments.

Doug, whose children attend the same school as Vera's, had approached Vera after a school meeting. "I heard you're going through a rough time. Do you want to get some coffee?" he had asked.

"No, I can't," she had said.

"Maybe some other time?" he had suggested.

"Maybe," she had mumbled.

Doug, obviously knowing about Vera's tenuous marital state, had called Vera a week later. "I got your number from the school directory," he had explained. "There's a great movie playing in your neighborhood. I'm going to the ten p.m. show Wednesday night. If you want, meet me there."

Tired of standing still for so long, Vera reaches for the raft that floats near her. She somehow manages to board it, lying with her face towards the sun. Maybe, she prays, the sun will turn me into a baked treat for the bugs flying above the water. Then, like a mummy in an Egyptian tomb, Vera places her arms across her chest and mentally returns to that fatal movie night.

Her children had known something was wrong. Although the impending divorce, compounded by her husband's refusal to leave the marital home until the ink on the divorce decree had dried, had made Vera more irritable than usual, on that particular Wednesday, she had snapped at everything her children had said and not said, done and not done. She had played Monopoly with her son, but she had not demonstrated her usual thirstiness to win. Vera could not analyze the pros and cons of building hotels on Boardwalk when all she could think about was Doug. She had helped her daughter squeeze anorexic Barbies into too small clothes, but her mind was on removing *her* clothes in front of a man for the first time in decades. To meet Doug at the movies could lead to many complications. What if someone saw them? What if he discovered that he did not like the touch of her skin or her lips? What if she gave way to a sexual desire that had lain dormant for years and got a disease or an unwanted pregnancy? Vera had weighed the what-ifs of staying home—spending another lonely night in the small fourth bedroom she had moved into after filing for divorce, watching more mindless television shows or rereading the same pages of her novel without comprehending a word, eating so many M&Ms that the caffeine kept her awake— with the what-ifs of going. Vera had gone.

The movie will never become "the special movie" of Doug and Vera because she has no memory of its title, characters, or plot. Instead, she only remembers sitting in the last row of the darkened theatre, oblivious to the two other people in the audience, and making-out with Doug as if she were a teenager on a first date. Vera's body had burned with desire, not shame, because she had not allowed herself to think of the consequences of her actions. She had refused to listen to her gut telling her that Doug, who had continued the make-out session after the movie in his red sports car with the black leather seats, was more the stereotypical "take 'em and leave 'em" guy than a real person with depth and possibility. Vera had not thought at all on that fateful Wednesday night; she had only felt, and those feelings had made her feel young and attractive and optimistic about herself and her future.

But the fire within Vera had quickly turned to ashes. Because Doug would rarely call her at home and neither she nor Doug owned a cell phone, their contact occurred only in the school parking lot where screaming kids, glad to be free for the day, and tense parents, anxious to get home, made intimate conversation impossible. The two did manage to set aside a weekly time—every Wednesday night at Doug's house—for sex. Vera became adept at lying in order to find excuses for her Wednesday absences. When her own lies occasionally tripped her, she remembered Dad's warning, "A liar needs a good memory."

Wednesday became the highlight of Vera's week, even though each Wednesday left Vera feeling more empty than full. She and Doug rarely talked, but instead did their communicating under the sheets—with him getting more than she received. He was a selfish lover, but that made him even more appealing to Vera. The more pleasure she gave him, the more he would need her. She could satisfy her sexual needs later in the privacy of her own room.

As a taciturn man, Doug revealed little about himself. Vera never learned what kind of books he favored, although stacks of old Sunday *New York Times* papers let her know that he did have an interest in world affairs. She knew he liked baseball because he took his children to games, but she did not know whether he gobbled a hot dog at the park or preferred the salty popcorn—or both. Did he stretch during the seventh inning like he did after sex, a sign that it was time for Vera to vacate his bed? Doug's eyes would light up if he saw any commercial for racing cars, but the same eyes became hooded when Vera suggested a Saturday night rendezvous. Although Vera knew little about Doug, she did know one fact: The Wednesday night girl would probably never become the Saturday night date.

Vera begins to fall asleep on the raft, but the squeaking of the gate awakens her. Startled by the sound—and praying that Doug has returned—Vera sits up, forgetting she is aboard a fragile rubbery raft in the middle of a pool. Just as she realizes that a breeze, not Doug, has tickled the gate into squealing, she topples into the water. When she tries to scream, she instead swallows mouthfuls of water. The chlorine burns her throat and her eyes. Vera feels like her five-year-old self, the little girl who had struggled in the undertow of the Atlantic Ocean until Dad had rescued her. Dad, however, is hundreds of miles away on this day of sunshine and darkness. Vera will have to save herself—if she chooses to do so.

And at this moment of panic and helplessness, she does opt for life. *I am not ready to go yet—not as this caricature I have let myself become*, Vera tells herself.

Vera pushes herself to the surface, opens her mouth to inhale the dry air, and swims toward the shallow end of the pool. Once safely on the deck, she wraps herself in her beach towel, sits on the chair Doug so recently vacated, and sees—she dries her eyes to make sure that what she sees is a reality and not an optical illusion—Doug's black datebook lying on the cement under the chair. In his haste to vacate the pool to prepare for his Saturday night girl, Doug inadvertently left Vera with this treasure.

The water Vera ingested in the pool turns to bile as Vera once again opens that malignant book and sees that Doug has added more names to the Barbara/Marci/Deb trilogy: Linda, Cynthia, Diane, Robin. The week-after-week litany of different names nauseates Vera. At one point, she gets the dry heaves. Fearing she might regurgitate her yogurt lunch, Vera leans over the thick bushes that separate her friends' house from the neighboring yard. Instead of gagging, however, Vera begins to sob. Each sob, like a ripple in the water, develops into another sob and another until Vera feels she will drown in her salty tears. On no page in the black book—not even on future Wednesdays—has Vera seen her name. Without her realizing it, Doug has deleted her, eliminated her, made her invisible.

Vera feels like those Russian nesting dolls Grandma once got her for a holiday present. With the turning of every page of Doug's black book, she shrinks, becoming as tiny and insignificant as the smallest doll in the set. Vera almost pities Barbara and Marci and Deb and all the others, but she knows it would be futile to warn them about Doug. Like her, they have to experience the violation of innocence to understand the primal pain that Vera now feels. They have to know what it means to want so much to be needed and held and loved that they are willing to sacrifice their integrity to achieve an illusion. They have to know what it is like to walk from the shallow end of their best friends' pool into the deep end that leads to oblivion.

The tears have stopped, as if Vera is no longer capable of

producing the most human of emotions—crying. The tears have stopped, but the anger—both at herself and at Doug—has begun. It bites at her toes and chews her feet, legs, and thighs. Still not satiated, it chomps her stomach and chest, arms and neck. The anger refuses to wait, but instead compels Vera to act. She grabs the black book, locks the gate—the only outside entrance to the backyard and pool—and enters the kitchen of her friends. Vera marches across the tiled floor, through the long hallway whose walls display pictures of family and friends (Vera ignores the one of her smiling as she poses like a model on the pool's diving board) and enters the office at the other end of the house. On the larger desk sits stacks of the husband's medical journals, while the smaller desk holds the wife's files filled with volunteer information for different charities. But it is the shelf of office supplies that fits snuggly between the two desks that calls out to Vera. After finding what she needs, Vera repeats her journey and again ends up in the backyard.

Stealing two of the larger, flatter rocks from the elaborate rock garden her friends had hired an artist to construct fills Vera with more guilt than her more heinous acts, but she has no time for morality. She instead concentrates on creating a sandwich of rock, black book, and rock, held together by the rubber bands she confiscated from the office. Vera marches across the deck to the opposite side of the pool, climbs the three steps leading to the diving board, walks to the middle of the board, sits with one leg dangling on either side, and drops the unappetizing sandwich into the pool. As the rocks drop to the bottom of the pool, they cause bubbles to appear—the same few bubbles that signal that someone has lost her battle with the water and is drowning. Vera watches as the water blurs the carefully written names in Doug's black book until all the names become one name: Vera. Then, the force of the water washes away all traces of the women, including Vera.

After covering the pool with its blue protective sheet, Vera returns to the kitchen, where she drinks glass after glass of water to sate her sudden thirst. She removes her still wet bathing suit, puts on shorts and a t-shirt, lies down on the couch in her friends' family room, and wraps herself in the afghan she had knitted for them as a gift.

Vera does not rush to the window to see Doug's blood-red sports car zoom into the driveway and barely miss knocking down the mailbox. She does not answer the frantic knocking at the door, even when Doug sounds as if he will huff and puff and blow the house down if Vera does not open the door and return the black leather book to him. She refuses to listen to Doug who, using his most resonant courtroom voice, shouts that she, not he, had initiated the Saturday afternoon pool fest. She, not he, had packed two outfits—one a casual blue pants suit, the other a dressier floral sundress—into her trunk "just in case" Saturday afternoon blossomed into Saturday night. She, not he, had brought false hopes and expectations to the pool. From the moment earlier that afternoon that Doug had gone into the kitchen to confirm his Saturday night date with one of the black book women, Vera had felt like the rape victim convinced she was responsible for her own violation. She will not give Doug another chance to ever make her feel that way again.

Vera lies on the couch and, hugging the afghan, begins the process of reclaiming her life as someone—as anyone—but a Wednesday night girl.

**About the author:**

Ronna has been fortunate to travel through life with three role models. Her Grandma taught her to get up and go about her business, no matter what troubles she may be experiencing. Ma assured her that "this too shall pass." Dad reminds her that a cud-chewing cow has a more sensible look than a gum-chewing girl, that hot Ovaltine in the winter and a cold chocolate phosphate in the summer will cure all problems, and that, in the words of Rudyard Kipling, it is good to "keep my head when all about you are losing theirs." All three encouraged her to read and dream, write and create.

As a part-time faculty member of the University of Pittsburgh's English Department, Ronna works as a consultant at the school's Writing Center. She also teaches Freshman Programs, a course that introduces students to the University and the city. Her work, both fiction and nonfiction, has appeared in "New Slang: A New Literary Voice by the Women and Girls of Pittsburgh" (online); *Quality Women's Fiction*; *Ghoti Online Literary Magazine*; *First Line Anthology*; *The Road to Elsewhere* (Scribes Valley Publishing, third place); *Welcome to Elsewhere* (Scribes Valley Publishing, second place); *Visiting Elsewhere* (Scribes Valley Publishing, third place); *When We Are* (Scribes Valley Publishing, second place); *SLAB: Sound and Literary Artbook*; *Pulse: Voices from the Heart of Medicine* (online and print); *AARP Bulletin* (online and print); *Healthy Roots* (Forbes Health Foundation and Hospice); *The Jet Fuel Review* (Lewis University's online literary journal); *Writer's Relief* (online); and the *Pittsburgh Post-Gazette*.

# SECOND PLACE

## AT YOUR GRAVE I STAND
©2013 by Carrie Rogers

Deborah and Shawn stared down at the gravestone. It was a simple marker poking out of the ground with only a small cross above the name to decorate it.

ROBERT S DUNHAM
Beloved Husband and Father
1978-2006

There were others like it lined up in rows upon rows, descending down the gentle incline of the hill. The neat order of the graves made it easier to forget what lay under each stone slab except for the one that mattered. Some, like Robert Dunham's, were squared, some rounded. Angel statues cried or plucked harps while watching over the dead. More angels or flowers were etched into the other stone markers. The gravestone of Robert Dunham, however, did not need such adornments.

Robert Dunham's grave was at the back row of the cemetery near a chain link fence. The fence protected the cemetery from drunkards and mischievous teenagers, and thick ivy grew around and through it. Branches from trees on the other side dangled over. Their now red and yellow leaves shivered in the autumn breeze, occasionally losing their hold and dripping into the cemetery. The chilly air hadn't affected the grass, which still grew thick and lush under a patchwork of dead leaves. A myriad of flower vases, standing vigil for loved ones gone, were the only signs of a living human presence.

Shawn cradled one such bouquet in his small hands, colorful enough to make up for the somber moment. His black suit looked awkward on him, his hunched shoulders betraying an otherwise reverent bearing and expression. He would rather have come in shorts and a T-shirt, his baseball uniform, anything other than the restrictive buttoned up collar and tie. But his mother had said this was what you wore at a cemetery, so he hadn't complained much. He wouldn't risk upsetting his mother enough to deter their annual visit.

The boy walked around the edge of the grave with steady, precise steps so as not to tread on the body buried underneath. This was his part in the ceremony they had followed for as long as he could remember. Shawn carefully squatted at the head of the grave to avoid mud and grass stains on the knees of his good suit and gently laid the bouquet across the front of the marker. Balancing on the balls of his feet, he pressed his hands together and bowed his head for a moment with his eyes squeezed shut, completely reverent in his prayer. A normally excited child, the stoic nature of his vigil showed just how much Shawn cared about the grave and the man underneath. He would do his best to honor the moment.

Deborah neither watched her son, nor observed the grave. She stood to the side with her back half to the grave, half to the garland fence. From her position she could see every grave in the cemetery almost down to the gates at the bottom of the hill. In her black dress and long overcoat, she folded her arms across her chest to protect herself from the cold—among other things. She kept her expression blank, if not reverent. Better to be here than the alternatives she thought of, but still she resented the yearly visits and how nervous they made her feel.

Deborah kept an eye out for anything out of the ordinary. They were the only ones visiting the cemetery that day, and that was how she liked it. She already felt as if someone was watching them, unseeing eyes judging and questioning their reason for being there. The feeling must have come naturally from standing in a cemetery, but that was no reason for her to lower her guard. Constant vigilance, that was the key. There was always someone watching just around the corner, even in a cemetery.

A gentle breeze jostled the leaves above them, drawing her attention. Deborah frowned at the distraction. Oak Prairie Cemetery was often empty. That was why Deborah chose it. In the years she had brought Shawn here, they had passed by other visitors coming or going, but no one who would stop and wonder at their business, no one who would make her worry. Leaves crunched on the ground behind her. She tried to hear beyond the wind and sense the presence of a potential threat.

Someone clearly stood behind them now, shuffling in the dead leaves. Deborah snapped her head in the direction of the noise, her already tense body becoming stiffer. She didn't see anyone, only a fat gray squirrel hunting in the grass.

Deborah allowed herself a sigh of relief, but her body failed to relax. It could have been anyone behind them, any visitor or thief or hoodlum. Constant vigilance. She would do better. For her son's sake, she would *have* to do much better.

Shawn pushed himself up when he finished his prayer. Deborah heard her son clap some dirt from his hands before moving to stand beside her, but she couldn't bring herself to watch him. Not when anyone could walk up that hill. They stood together in silence, the boy staring at the grave and Deborah at everything else.

"Mom," Shawn finally asked, "how did Daddy die?"

Deborah never talked about Shawn's father, and there were no pictures of him in their apartment. The memories were often too painful. The boy brought the subject of his father up once in a while, only to upset and frustrate his mother to the point where

Shawn didn't ask about him anymore. But Deborah had seen the questions in his eyes whenever a sports season started or they spotted a father and son walking down the street. Shawn would look up at her for a moment then quickly glance away before he said anything to divulge his curiosity.

He wanted answers, and his curiosity wasn't something that would go away in time. Deborah knew this. She had always known Shawn needed to be told something. So this was their compromise, their tradition. This was the one day out of the year devoted to his father, when they visited Robert Dunham's grave and Shawn could ask all the questions he wanted.

A mother was enough for Shawn the rest of the year, but Deborah could see as the days drew closer how anxious he became. As other children waited for Christmas, Shawn hardly contained himself those days before they dressed up in their best, most uncomfortable clothes and drove out to Oak Prairie. It was a treat for the boy, as longed for as any present, well worth enduring the solemn decorum and constricting clothes. Shawn asked his questions, and Deborah had all the answers.

How did Daddy die? It was the question he led with last year.

"It was a car accident," she answered matter-of-factly. "He was on his way home from work when another car ran a red light and hit him."

"Where did he work? What did he do?"

"He was a scientist. He designed prosthetic limbs, fake arms and legs for people who had lost theirs."

At this, Deborah chanced a look down at her son and smiled at what she saw. Shawn now stared ahead at the words inscribed in stone, his mind hard at work. She could imagine what decisions his ponderings would lead to. He memorized all her responses, no doubt. Her words shaped his understanding of the vacant hole in his family. Shawn would grow up loving science because his father had. Maybe he'd even become a scientist himself, like a doctor or an engineer. He would work hard at school to build and maintain any connection he could with his father's spirit. She had made a good choice.

"Did he play any sports?" Shawn asked, looking back up at her. This was another question from last year. What had she told him?

"He played basketball in high school and a little in college." Deborah couldn't remember the rest of last year's answer.

"What was his favorite color? Was it red?"

"No. It was green." After all, the boy couldn't be *exactly* like Robert Dunham.

"He was funny, though, right? I mean, not goofy. Sometimes people say I'm goofy, but he was funny. Wasn't he?"

"He knew some good jokes," Deborah answered, nodding and trying her best to smile. Something moved in the corner of her eye, but it was only another leaf falling. "He liked puns. People would groan at his jokes, but I enjoyed listening to them. I'd tell him they were awful and he'd just tell me another one."

"And was he strong? A real man has to be super strong, like those wrestlers on TV!" Shawn flexed his arms like a body builder for his mother as a demonstration.

Deborah watched him, and her fake smile faltered. "Yes," she whispered, remembering. "He was very strong."

Her son didn't notice the change in her demeanor. He continued asking questions left and right: Did Daddy ever have a dog? Where did he live while growing up? Did he hate doing the dishes too? What would he have done if Ethan Marshal called *him* a sissy in front of all his friends? He paused when he couldn't think of another question right away, then he stumbled over his words when they finally came to him, rushing to get them out of his mouth. He had all day to quiz his mother and to hear anecdotes of the past, but he wanted to get the most of it while he could.

Shawn asked his questions at random, constantly shifting his gaze from the gravestone to his mother and back again. Some were mere wonderings of a boy wanting to know his father. The rest sparked from events of the past year only a father could answer. Through her, Shawn sought his father's approval and did what he could to be like the man he imagined his father to be. Chris Yanish's dad took him to the ballpark every summer. Daddy liked playing in batting cages, didn't he?

Deborah did her best to answer every question. There were some things she wouldn't say about the man, but every answer she gave she tried to memorize just as carefully as Shawn did. She would have to recite them again next year and the year after that and elaborate on the answers.

Shawn's next pause between questions lingered. He looked from the gravestone to his mother. When he spoke again, his young voice stumbled with hesitation. "Mom, why don't we have the same name as him?"

It was the first time Shawn asked that particular question, but Deborah had been expecting it. He would have asked it sooner or later, and she had made sure she would be ready with an answer. "Well, I kept my name because of my work, and we gave you my last name to make your grandpa happy. There aren't too many Tatmans in the world. You should be proud to have it for a last name."

"I guess," Shawn grumbled.

In a rare moment of trust, Deborah turned her back on the rest of the world and knelt down beside her son. Her stomach clenched at the thought of leaving herself exposed, but some things were more important. She pointed at the gravestone. "But see, look there. I did name you after him."

Shawn scowled, searching for any hint as to what his mother meant. He must have noticed the S shoved between the engraved first and last name; Shawn jerked his head from Deborah to the gravestone and back again. "Really?" he exclaimed, surprised and pleased with the sudden revelation.

The satisfaction faded quickly, though. Shawn looked away from both his mother and the grave as he considered something more. "That's good," he said slowly, "but at least I look like him, right, Mom?"

Deborah didn't think much of the boy's question at first—it was just another one in a series that needed answering—but when she glanced across at her son, ready with an automatic response, the question wrapped around her mind. Her planned words slipped away as she looked at Shawn, *really* looked at him.

Shawn had a round face and a small nose, closely resembling her. His hair was the same honey blond. But then Deborah looked at his eyes. Hers were brown, dark and smooth like chocolate, but Shawn had blue eyes.

She remembered those eyes. Deborah reached to touch Shawn's face with one hand, hoping to somehow wipe the memory away. His eyes brought out other features; features she wished she'd long forgotten. She remembered his father on that cold night long ago. She remembered his heavy weight pressing down on her, smothering her, as he stared at her with those same eyes. She remembered the sting of his fists and another, sharper thing.

The stiffness left Deborah's body and the sudden rush of nausea threatened to choke her. The rest of the world faded away, leaving her in that place and time. Those blue eyes striped away all her defenses. Her hand started to tremble against Shawn's face at the thought of him, her breathing growing more ragged, her eyes blurring. The memory consumed her. She felt cold. So cold.

"Mom? Are you all right?"

Deborah shook her head. She would never tell him about his real father. He didn't deserve the burden and pain of such a secret. It was her responsibility. She would protect her son from that secret so it could never hurt him. She had to keep it together for Shawn's sake.

Instead of touching his face, Deborah grabbed Shawn's arms and held them firmly. She clung to him as he continued to watch her and wait for her answer. "No," Deborah told her son, drawing a deep breath. "No, you look nothing like him. You are your mother's son, through and through." She would believe nothing less.

Shawn's expression drooped, crestfallen. Deborah wondered for a moment if she had said the right thing. Over the years, she had carefully crafted a father her son could be proud of. Maybe, just this once....

Deborah opened her mouth to speak, but then Shawn nodded to himself as though her answer would be enough. Well, if he could live with her answer for now, so could she. Deborah released her grip on her boy. He leaned over and hugged his mother. Deborah pulled him into her arms and held him tight.

She was a coward, creating an imaginary father for a boy who had none, at least none she wanted to think about. Shawn was her son and no one else's. But she had realized after some time that she wouldn't always be enough for him, so she had gone out to find someone who would be. She had searched through a number of graveyards until she found a name that fit her needs, someone the right age and far enough away to avoid inconvenient questions.

Robert Dunham gave Shawn something she couldn't. It wasn't a perfect plan, inventing a father for her son to look up to and using someone else's grave to perpetuate the lie. So many things could go wrong. Shawn would figure it out, given time. But it was for the best for as long as it lasted. Better he not know about the monster that, even after all these years, still haunted Deborah's dreams.

Deborah leaned back so her hug relaxed into a hand hold. She squeezed his hand before she stood. "Are you ready to go?"

Usually, when Deborah stopped answering his questions, Shawn started talking to Robert Dunham. He told his 'father' stories about his life and concerns. If nothing else, Robert was a good listener. Today, Deborah held tightly to Shawn's hand. He looked back at the grave one last time before nodding.

Deborah smiled, her lips trembling as she tried not to cry. She drew another breath and settled into a more convincing and heartfelt smile. She knew what her son was giving up just to make her feel better. "Come on," she said, regaining some of her confidence. "Let's get you some hot chocolate."

With her spirits up, Shawn cheered as well. "Can we have pie, too? With ice cream?"

"Whatever you want. Today, it's all for you."

Deborah pulled Shawn's head against her hip and ruffled his hair. He had insisted on combing it neat and straight for the special occasion. Shawn tried to escape her hold on him, and Deborah reached down and tickled his side, resulting in a burst of laughter from her sweet and beautiful boy. It was all for the best.

They started walking. As Shawn's thoughts turned to future delights, Deborah kept her eyes on the trees. Once she was convinced no one was there to jump out at them, she looked back at the grave one last time. She wondered what kind of man Robert Dunham had been when he was alive, if he *did* play basketball in high school or if his favorite color *was* green. Was he a kind man? Would he have approved of what she was doing? She wished she had really known him and what kind of father he had been.

Sometimes, when they weren't visiting the grave and she was trying to come up with answers for Shawn's questions, Deborah wondered if Robert Dunham couldn't be someone special for *her* as well. The real Robert Dunham buried in that grave may have a wife who visited some other time of the year, but *this* Robert—the one she made up stories about for Shawn—he could be hers. She could pretend he had been a good man and husband. She could imagine being safe with him. Maybe it would help.

Shawn tugged on her arm and Deborah faced forward. She smiled down at Shawn now that old memories were safely put away. They walked down the hill together toward hot chocolate with pie and ice cream. They continued on together, leaving Oak Prairie Cemetery for another year.

**About the Author:**

Carrie Rogers lives in Minnesota where she works as a freelance editor and proofreader. She is actively involved in the diverse literary community in the Twin Cities. She writes poetry, short prose, and speculative fiction. Her work has previously been published in Studio One, The Drabbler, and Toasted Cheese Literary Journal.

# THIRD PLACE

## THE WORLD BEYOND THE SHELL
©2013 by Alex G. Friedman

I park in my apartment garage and turn off the car before it occurs to me that I might have left my crab, Claud, at the grocery store. Had I even brought Claud? The warm haze of pleasant distraction that had carried my spirit during the drive home from the store slowly dissipates. I'm in for it now. I am too young for these great scientific responsibilities.

Twenty-four is too young.

Too spontaneous.

Too horny.

My source of distraction is a girl named Vicky. I met her two weeks ago during a midnight run to the store. Claud needed food. I stood at the grocery store counter as Vicky checked the cat food cans through the laser scanner. I tried to figure out how to talk to her, which was hard as she was very pretty. Her hair was dyed and cut short to highlight her eyes. She scanned cans faster than I could pull them out of my cloth shopping bag. I had decided to stock up. I didn't really know how much he was supposed to eat, because I never paid enough attention to what they put in his tank at the lab. I dumped the rest of the bag into my folded arm so that she wouldn't have to slow down. She saw me check her name badge and smiled at me.

"What's your kitty's name?" Vicky asked. She clacked her white polka dotted nails rhythmically across the metal counter as she waited for me to prepare my credit card.

"Claud," I said.

"Aw, I love boy cats. What color is he?" She asked. She had a very nice smile.

"He's melon red with white on his underbelly and legs," I said.

"He's a big guy, huh?" She said.

"Yeah, I think he might be growing again." I said. I *had* noticed he was molting and growing another shell. This was the third time this week. He was already able to reach the radio dial with his pincer from inside his tank. He seems to prefer NPR.

"Well, have a nice night!" She said.

I packed my bag. "I'll try!" I said with a grunt as I hoisted Claud's food. Smooth.

From that brief exchange, I knew where I'd be shopping for the foreseeable future. I tried to figure out what kind of music she probably liked. Something acoustic, I figured. I drove home, preoccupied with infatuation, just as I did every other night for the past two weeks.

I enter my apartment and check his tank. My heart sinks. He is not there. He'd left out his map book. He seems to have torn off some of the pages with his pincers. I'll have to buy him a new one. I mentally retrace my steps. I am almost sure that he gave me the slip at the grocer's. I put down my shopping bag and walk back to my car. I was stupid to bring him along. I don't remember if he'd had to convince me or if I had thought the idea clever.

I'm an intern at a deep sea medical research firm. When Claud was brought to the surface a few months ago, dragged out of the Arctic Ocean along with a dozen other strange deep-sea specimens, he wasn't expected to survive. A deep-sea crab isn't *supposed* to survive on the shallow, depressurized surface. But he did. That was the first miracle.

Then it turned out he didn't need to be underwater all the time, either. He climbed up the filtration system and snipped through the chicken-wire lid of his aquarium with his long, scissor-shaped claws. We followed the wet claw marks on the floor and found him sitting on top of a Popular Mechanics magazine on my desk. That's when I named him Claud. I thought I saw Claud's beady little eyes scanning the text on the page he was sitting on when I lifted him and gently sat him back in his tank. I was careful not to invite the wrath of his pincers, but he didn't even try to pinch. He looked at me and fizzed a tiny whistle through his jaws.

I can only assume this was the deep-sea crab speak equivalent of *I was reading that.*

The next morning, I was horrified to find on the day's schedule that Claud had been marked for dissection. I probably would have decided to take him home at that point anyway, but when I looked at his tank I noticed he was drawing and annotating isosceles triangles in the algae that grew on the aquarium glass. So, I scooped Claud out of his tank and put him in a wastepaper basket (I cleaned it first) and then I took him home.

So that's why I secretly have a sentient deep-sea crab living in an aquarium on the coffee table beside my couch.

Anyhoo...

I make it a point to talk to Vicky whenever I go to the grocer, which thankfully is quite often due to Claud's growing appetite. Vicky tells me about her latest painting, or about the picnics she goes on with her Grandmother, and I tell her how big and smart Claud is getting. Of course, she thinks Claud is a cat, but I still feel that our conversations are pleasant and honest. I wish I didn't have to leave out the stories about his reading habits.

I am driving back the the grocery store. I brought a picture of me and Claud, a travel aquarium, and a few of Claud's favorite books on theoretical mathematics. I had hoped to ask Vicky out the next time I saw her, but I figure this probably isn't going to be the ideal time.

I run to the big glass front doors of the market and they part in front of me with a *whoosh*. The light in the store is very blue and cold and artificial. I see Vicky watching me with concern as I hurry in. I probably look upset.

I say, "Have you seen Claud?"

She asks, "Your kitty?"

I say, "Yes. Well, he's a crab, but my other descriptions were fairly accurate."

I look about the small grocery store. There are only ten aisles, only so many places a crab might hide unnoticed.

She says, "What do you mean your kitty is a crab?"

I say, "A crustacean, I mean. Long legs with snippy parts."

"Ah," she says, "it eats cat food?"

I say, "Yes, have you seen him?"

She looks around and then shakes her head.

"What kind of crab is he?" she asks.

I reach into my pocket to show her the picture of Claud but something has snipped my pants pocket wide open at the seam.

I say, "I thought I had a picture with me to show you, but..."

And that's when we hear the squeal of tires and we turn around to see Claud speeding away in my car.

**About the author:**

Alex Friedman was described in a eulogy as a fictitious character created as part of an elaborate hoax. He writes, works, and studies at Miami University. Alex would like to thank Tamara Guirado for her encouragement on "The World Beyond the Shell."

# A HAUNTED HOUSE
©2013 by Mary Smith

It's cold today and the wind is blowing from the north again. I get out of the car as a coil of air gathers up dried leaves and tosses them at me, plastering me with dust and pelting me with tiny pebbles from the driveway. I slam the car door and dash to the back steps of the house, looking to have some refuge from the blustery season's sting and the next-door neighbors' stare. One person, whose house is to the left, is pulling aside her curtain to better see what's going on at the vacant house. Small town carefulness at work here, I think.

The empty house was my childhood home while my parents were alive, and now it belongs to me. My parents have been gone for some time and I have come home to tend to the issues they left me. I have arranged for the old place to be torn down and the lot cleared to sell. This chilly morning, I am here to make sure that everything is as it should to be for the demolition.

The electricity, as well as the water and gas, was terminated weeks ago so there will be no electrocutions, no explosions, or geysers of costly city water shooting into the air to mark the day of destruction in anyone's memory—or my pocketbook.

Grasping the handle on the old screen door—one I've held so many times—that opens on the rear porch, I prepare to go in. As expected, the door hangs on the first pull. having swollen from the humidity brought on by the cool fall weather. Dad never did get the door planed so it wouldn't do that, and we had just learned to live with it.

As I yank quick and hard, the door comes loose, and I step onto the floorboards of the back porch. The porch has never been any more level than the screen and sits at a slant towards the door. Dad told us once that the porch wasn't original to the house and had been added some years later. That explained the ill-fitting room and why nothing round stayed where you put it. I've noticed over the years that old houses are frequently like this: odd and misshapen.

My shoes thump across the wood floor as I walk into the house. The sound reminds me of Dad's heavy, clunky work boots as he walked out the back door leaving for work. He worked almost every day until it was well past dark. Dad never missed a day of work that I can remember.

Once inside the house I can see that the first bedroom is empty except dust moats, disturbed by the door, floating in the air. Light filters through smudged and marked panes in the tall wooden window casements. I see that one or two have glass missing, but it doesn't matter one iota since the windows are going with everything else to the dump.

The kitchen is to my left and I turn to go in. For just an instant I'm startled, thinking I see my mother standing at the kitchen stove, surrounded by her pots and pans. She was always cooking and stirring and mixing something in that room. The kitchen was the center of action during the holidays and always the warmest room in the house in winter. The old Viking gas range is long gone and the space heater that sat in one corner has been removed to the thrift store.

Taking a deep breath, I walk swiftly through the cold kitchen, its warmth sapped not only from the weather but from lack of human presence. I step into the living room just through the next door, stopping abruptly on the threshold. Memories engulf me as I stand there in another time. Christmases, Halloweens, Thanksgivings, and the family good times—as well as the bad— whirl in competition for my attention. A good deal of sorrow and happiness was experienced in this whole house, but mostly in this one room. Family battles were fought here, hugs and even paddlings were given when needed. Tears were shed over lost toys, pets, and boyfriends. Laughter was shared as we opened presents on Christmas day or watched a game on television and reveled in the joy of a winning team.

Sights, smells, and sounds whirl around me in a confusion of images and sensations remembered. My attention, however, is brought back to the present by the sight across the room of an old piece of furniture sitting in a corner. Dad's old green recliner, missed somehow when the thrift store people took everything else away. Maybe it was just too old and worn for them to try to sell in their store.

I can see my dad sitting there in the last years of his life, a shadow of the man I had grown up with, shrunken due to age and illness and grief at Mom's passing a few years before. He became uncommunicative and childlike, and when he passed I realized it was a blessing because he had been suffering so.

With his presence still close the urge is strong to sit in the chair one more time. Bits of cotton and the tops of metal springs poke through the fake leather cover and there are rips all over the back where large green buttons once were sewn. I sneaked many moments in that chair when I was younger, usually waiting until everyone had gone to bed and no one—especially Dad—would know that I had propped my feet in his chair while I ate popcorn and watched all night fright movies. I think that he knew, but didn't mind as long as no damage was done and the evidence would not show the next day. In the daytime nobody sat there but him and that old cat who passed a long time ago and was buried under the old mesquite tree. What a shame that old tom can't be buried close to Dad at the cemetery. But who knows? Maybe they're somewhere together right now anyway.

Drawing a deep breath of strength, I turn and go back the way I came. Through the kitchen, bedroom, porch, and out the old screen door, letting it close behind me for the last time, shutting inside another time and place.

I pull my coat and scarf tighter around my throat and shoulders and, leaning into the November wind, I make it to the car and get in. I turn the key and the motor roars to life and I back out of the drive none too carefully. The curtain in the house to the left doesn't move again, curiosity having been satisfied.

*I leave behind an old house filled with childhood memories and one old, green recliner that the contractor will take to the dump along with everything else that no longer has a use,* I think to myself. *Or maybe one of the crew will decide the old chair will serve a purpose in their garage or even a hunter's country cabin.*

At the end of the road I brake for the stop sign and I glance into the rearview mirror for one last look. Standing there at the back of the house on the porch steps are my mom and dad, exactly as I remember them when I was a child. Wishfully, as our eyes meet they wave and, although it may look to anyone observing that I've finally lost it, I wave back and mouth the words, "So long, see ya later, and I love you." Hesitantly, I release the brake, turn on the blinker, and make the corner down Llano Street and then left to the main highway. I think to myself as the car speeds down the highway out of town, *you can't tell me there are no such things as ghosts. I just visited a haunted house and saw some!*

**About the author:**

Here it comes, fall and then winter soon after. Love this time of year. When it's cold outside that's when I do my best writing; when the best ideas seem to pop into my head and at the strangest times. Things are slow at work because old people don't like to move in the cold seasons, thank goodness. This means that I can sit and jot down ideas off and on all day and then write them up when I get home.

So here I am, better than yesterday and not as good as tomorrow.

# THE CHERRY TREE
©2013 by Rachel Worrall

It poured for four days and a lake accumulated outside the front door of 2 Blethers, covering so great an area that they were unable to get to their car parked on the road that ran perpendicular to Blethers, without hoisting their trousers up and wearing waterproof shoes. Sarah and Michael were ill-prepared for a flood. Not realising that their house was in danger they had not taken up the offer of sandbags from the council, nor did it occur to them to remove their new plum coloured hall carpet. The water level of the lake, after all, remained constant for three days. But then the drain, just outside and to the right of their front door, backed up, and the water frothed, swirling with bubbles and tumbling pink petals until it eventually broke over their threshold and not long after the man from the council was standing on it in his Wellies explaining that the drain was a private drain—a drain that was their responsibility as the owners of the house.

Sarah and Michael had just enough cash left between them to call out the cheapest drain cleaner they could find. The water by then was at least a foot deep in the hallway and covered most of the way to the second step on the stairs. It left filthy stains where it slopped against the new and thoughtfully chosen royal-blue paintwork. Pink blossoms stuck to the walls. Michael, who had sweated over the paintwork, flicked his right fore-fingernail against his left and unable to relieve his frustration in this way, punched his fist against the wall, too angry to speak. Sarah made the call and reported that the drain cleaner was so busy given the current weather he was only able to fit them in after the weekend.

In the meantime, Dan the drain cleaner had given them some advice. They took all their towels, even the gold monogrammed aqua ones Sarah had given Michael as a wedding present, and built bulky dams around the kitchen and living room doors in a desperate attempt to prevent the water from ruining the oak effect laminate flooring they'd had put down over the original slate. Every hour they were awake they bailed out the hallway as best they could with what buckets and pans they had. They cursed the amorphous soap suds of pearlescent pink petals sliding between their hands, buckets and legs. The water though continued to rise, now entirely covering the second step.

Dan arrived at last, and nodded in sympathy at the fact that their dams had failed and they had had to pull up the hall carpet and throw away most of the laminate flooring and didn't know how they were going to pay for a new lot. He set off his drain cleaning machine, all the while whistling as he admired the cherry blossoms that had formed rims round both of his Wellies. He turned to find the tree that they had come from and stood admiring it.

It truly was a beautiful tree, tall, its limbs held patiently aloft. Though the rain had crumpled much of its blossoms, it remained as fine a sight as a wedding cake. Dan realised he must be looking at Percy Mason's garden. When Dan was a child, Percy's dahlias had won prizes each year in Kirkside's garden festival, while Annie Mason took away the cake trophy more than once. Dan's parents were always trying to beat the Masons. His father said that Percy's secret was that he collected his own manure from the farms and did not rely on what they sold in Sterns. Tom, the Mason's son had been a few years above Dan in school. Every year when they were in the Junior School Tom brought in a birthday cake with fresh cream and chocolate icing, big enough for everyone to have a slice. Tom, though, was a bit of a loner like his dad, Dan recalled.

Dan looked over the privet hedging beyond the tree and took in the potatoes and the stakes for the peas, the apple and pear trees shading a large pond, rose bushes in beds curving around the lawn and though they were not yet in bloom he could see the bamboo stakes waiting to support the dahlias and sweet peas in the summer. He had always been told that Percy Mason's garden was a wonder and he was pleased that this morning's job had brought him to it. Even though the patch looked ill-tended now, with the stakes bent at all angles and weeds growing between them, he could imagine what a glory it could have been. He would tell his folks he'd seen it. Their rivalry as a young couple had mellowed and they'd be sad to know from the state of the place that Percy wasn't getting into his garden as much as he used to.

Sarah and Michael paid in cash, which made Dan cheerier still and as he was leaving he decided to do them a favour and remind them of the things they should not be putting down their drains—including pasta in the kitchen drain, especially pasta. The number of times he had to get out of bed because of spaghetti, if only they knew. But instead of being grateful Michael would not meet his eye while Sarah explained that they had not put anything down their drain and had not the flowers blocked it?

Dan shrugged. "Anything will block a drain if you put enough of it down it but I very much doubt the cherry blossoms 're the problem here. There's only one tree, anyway. But if you're worried about it, buy a drain cover—you can get them from Sterns for about five quid. The previous owners likely had one as I've never heard of any flooding up here before now." With that he climbed back into his cab.

Cherry blossoms. Michael and Sarah had not known the petals were cherry blossoms. And all from the tree across the way. Well, they would see about that. They knew their rights; they would post a note through that old man's door. It was about time he sorted out his garden.

It was Percy who planted the tree. He was always growing things, being both curious and determined and seeming to have, anyway, a natural affinity for it. It used to be a great joke when his wife Annie laughed that she'd popped the question else Percy would have married a plant, a great joke that is until their son Tom, in a fit of adolescent pique, said one day that they would all have better off if he had done so.

The cherry tree came from the cherry that grew, famously, at the entrance to the long drive up to Kirkside's castle and one day in spring, on his way to school when he was fourteen, Percy found a small broken branch from it on the path. From this the tree grew so well that Percy was eventually able to plant it, on the day he and Annie moved in, in the corner of their new garden which backed onto Blethers.

Percy chose the place for his tree with care. He did not want to block the light entering either his house nor of the two houses at the back on Blethers and limiting the area he would one day use for a vegetable plot. He wanted to avoid low-spreading branches causing a nuisance to passersby by hanging over his privet hedge. He was lucky that the tree, with careful pruning, grew tall and thin. And that it had the most beautiful, pink double blossoms, like petticoats of tulle.

The street Percy and Annie moved onto, on Sandwith Lane, was a new development of houses on a new street, part of the council's plan to create affordable homes for returning servicemen and their families throughout the town. True, the houses were not as grand as the new-builds elsewhere but there was something about this row of brick terraced homes, all roofed with slate from the quarry a few miles away, all with large back gardens as well as small front gardens, each with large front and back windows and each with two large and one smaller bedrooms and a standalone kitchen, dining room and living room downstairs. Percy and Annie Mason stood a little taller to be house owners on such a street.

The butterscotch coloured paint was still clammy when they moved in. They were both desperate to do so; it was already 1947 and ever since the end of the war, when they were married, and Annie made Percy move to Kirkside from the outlying village of

Lorton Moor (though he would work there as a miner for some years yet), they had been squeezed in with her parents. There had already been a big falling out between Percy and her folks once. No one wanted another.

Percy and Annie's was at the far end of the street. Not only did it boast a wooden decorative peak on the roof at the front (to match the one on the house at the other end), but it had easily the finest view. For Sandwith Lane was built on the town's old drying greens where the land fell away on two sides to the river Coburn, leaving the horizon clear for a vista that took in the entire town, the two rivers, the church, the town hall, the old textile mill and the low hills to the west.

The house was rather bare at first, just the two of them and a mattress. Their family, neighbours and friends did not see them go needy, however, and they were almost overwhelmed in their first few years by donations and hand-me-downs. Later, most of the things for their baby boy, Tom, were gifted in this way, the town teeming with toddlers at that period. The only objects considered to be of real value in the house were Annie's china set which she bought piece by piece, week by week, from Sterns on Main Street, and her organ, a present from Percy, which she would play in the evenings when there would be a singalong, doubling as practice for church on Sunday.

Percy eventually left the coal mine and, building on the work he had done as first aid man for Kirkside's Rugby League club, he trained for the ambulance service. He also took on labouring work, spending his days off one summer breaking rocks for the new motorway. A good chunk of this work paid for Annie's organ. So in the early years of their lives on Sandwith, beyond planting the cherry tree, Percy did not have much time for the back garden beyond thinking to and from work of how he would lay it out when he had the money and the time.

Nevertheless he did what he could. He let Annie use their wedding money to buy the linens she wanted for the house but asked for a small amount to be kept back for himself, explaining that he wanted to make a start with some potatoes and some dahlias.

Perhaps because the tree was the first thing Percy ever put into the garden, perhaps because it grew so quickly into something so majestic, it became the garden's most talked about piece, notwithstanding the fact that it was the dahlias that won all the prizes. A neighbour took Percy and Annie's photo by it when it was first planted, Annie in her apron and slippers and Percy's arm, long and thin like the rest of him, about her shoulders, and after that it became the backdrop for all family photos, one of Tom pulling a face on his first day at school; one of Tom and Annie before Tom's wedding, Annie looking nervous in her hat and gloves, Tom grinning with his father's lopsided smile; Percy and Annie on their silver and ruby anniversaries, the first holding between them a cake Tom had insisted on buying for them and which was quietly consigned to the dustbin, the second posing with a red velvet cake Annie made herself about which Percy said "It's the best yet, love"; loads of Tom's kids, doing hand stands against the tree; posing with new bicycles beside it at Christmas; standing up smart and straight on their own first day at school, all these photos coming ultimately to rest on Annie's sideboard.

As Percy and Annie aged, their neighbours aged with them. Annie used to joke that the only way people left Sandwith was in a coffin. Percy and Annie knew all of their neighbours they still lived amongst, many of whom were school or family friends. If Kirkside was a monopoly board and Percy and Annie's house on one corner, they knew the occupier of each house on the sides stretching away from them. They knew the people who lived on Blethers and the people who lived on Layart Street perpendicular to Blethers and because of Tom they knew all of their now grown children as well. Annie's closest cousins lived on Layart and *their* neighbours were close friends of Percy's parents. Annie and Percy's house was like the church hall on a Sunday, a place for people to meet, have a cup of tea and a bite to eat, and sometimes stay the night; the grandkids seemed always to be there, as did Margaret from next door chattering away through the blue plumes of her cigarette smoke, and Bill, come to talk to Percy about keeping the snails away from his cauliflowers. And the years of piecemeal buying for the garden as for the house meant that each was finally coming into its own.

In time Annie was no longer able to play the big organ in church as she couldn't manage the steps up to it. Percy continued to work until he saw he needed to retire to look after her. Those days, though, were still good days. In the summer their neighbour's grandchildren would play in Percy's garden with Tom's children; Percy was usually at work among his dahlias, squirting them all on hot days with a hose, standing back under the cherry tree to admire his work. These were the garden's glory days, days when it gave back as much as it was given in colour, scent, full green growth, pale yellow potatoes, sweet pears, soft-bellied plums, flowers for the table and apples for Annie's pies and standing keeping a watchful eye above it all was the cherry tree wearing its new growth with quiet pride.

Then Annie's cousin, their neighbour, died and not long afterwards her widowed husband moved in with his daughter on the other side of town. The friends of Percy's parents also passed away. Tom and his family moved out of town to Beckwith when he took the headship at the school there. And Kirkside itself was changing; many young couples from out of town, further afield than before, even from the midlands and down south, filled up the new developments on what had once been farmland or common pasture on the outskirts. The great chimney on the cotton mill was demolished and the building itself turned into apartments and enterprise units.

A supermarket chain bought up the site where the old livestock auction stood, forcing Main Street's two family butchers and three family bakers to struggle on or close their doors. Tom had only ever bought bread for his parents and his own family from Martins and Tom kept shaking his head every time he walked past the now empty store. With the demutalisation of the building societies, bank branches first flourished, then as deregulation came in and mergers took place, the banks and their cash machines began to disappear. Percy and Annie themselves did not have many years left. Annie became sick with breast-cancer and people stopped staying over and dropping in for a cup of tea. Percy thought they were staying away because of Annie's cancer and grew silently angry at them for it until, at her funeral, he realised that people had been staying away because they, too, had passed away. It was always Annie who had kept tabs on people, you see.

And had Annie been alive she would have gone round when Sarah and Michael moved in taking with her a set of her freshly baked rock buns and an invitation to drop by. But she'd been dead seventeen years, by then, and Percy had withdrawn further into himself after her death. He himself spent so much time at the hospital these days that he was not always at home and it was quite a few years since he had felt strong enough to walk down to the bottom of the garden, when he might have seen the flood developing and gone around to help.

Sarah and Michael had lived on Blethers for about eight months when their house flooded, which was also as long as they had lived together. Both had worked until recently at Forville's new leisure pool where Sarah managed the cafeteria and Michael was a lifeguard. Their affair had started when the pool had opened eighteen months prior—

"We always knew they were at it cos the door to the freezer room was closed," said a girl who also worked in the kitchen. At Forville's secondary school, Michael had secretly fancied Sarah, who was a couple of years older than he, while Sarah, not finding Michael attractive at school on account of his ginger hair, changed her mind when she saw how nicely he had filled out. Shortly before the move into their small cottage, they were married in Vegas as, they liked to say, by Elvis.

Both were predisposed to flirtation by the boredom that the hours at the not very full pool brought on. Sarah found herself unable to stop herself finding ways to touch Michael whenever he came into the cafeteria for his bacon butties. For his part Michael was gratified by all the attention, Sarah's pert breasts and the fact she smelled good. He liked to say to her how he knew she was in the kitchen in the morning even though he had not seen her come in because he could smell her perfume on the breeze through the open windows of the pool.

Neither gave any thought to being found out. When they were thrown out by their spouses, summarily divorced and forced to abandon a beloved child apiece, they clung to each other. Ostracised by friends and family, both saw making a go of it as the best way to stick it to their detractors. And so they moved to Kirkside where they considered the house on Blethers to be perfect: a tiny two-up two-down cottage dating back to the turn of the century, on a quiet street and with a pub just around the corner. "Sorted," Michael had said and they had hugged each other in relief. Now they only needed to find work.

At this, Sarah had good luck. The Riverside Hotel, on the meadowy bank of the town's larger river, was looking for a catering manager and hired her within a week. But Michael was not so lucky. He waited four months for something to come up, making almost daily trips to the Job Centre, his growing frustration expressing itself in angry outbursts of thrown crockery and the shooting of rabbits in the lane with his air rifle. Their first real argument occurred when Sarah cancelled Michael's gym membership to pay for replacement plates.

In the end Michael followed the advice of the Job Centre's staff and took a position as sales clerk in a mobile phone store in town. All in all, though they were both being paid about as much as before, they found they were not able to go out as often to the pubs, something they had both looked forward to as Michael had been banned from all the pubs in Forville for starting fights, nor could they go on city breaks to Barcelona, Rome and Paris as often as they were used to, having no remaining savings and child support and legal fees to pay. On top of all that Sarah discovered that all the romantic weekends away with Michael, including that of their wedding in Vegas, had been paid for on several credit cards, money which they were now obliged to pay back.

So Sarah and Michael wrote their note and posted it through Percy's door, but they did nothing when they did not receive a reply, other troubles once again overtaking them, the drain, which was functioning normally, not being one of them. Sarah had been promised a pay raise which was not forthcoming. Michael and Sarah had paid off some of their debt but at Christmas they found themselves compelled to spend more on their absent children and on each other than was prudent and at the start of January discovered they were in a slightly worse financial position than ever before. Neither of them was to blame more than the other but, silently and then not so silently, they took it out on each other and by the beginning of the spring, Michael was sleeping on the sofa.

Then it rained. And the outside drain backed up again and this time the water did not wait but during the night started to come in over the threshold and down the hallway before they had a chance to take up the replacement plum coloured hall carpet and protect the replacement oak effect laminate flooring and move the cream sofa they had agonised over along with the glass coffee table, two matching cream chairs, as well as the round pine dining set with four cream padded chairs, upstairs. The water this time reached the third step of the hall staircase. They reported smelling gas from the living room fire but the gas man said that he couldn't fix it until the water situation was resolved, then turned their gas off at the mains.

They saw the cherry blossoms once again swimming about their doorstep. The flowers had failed to get past their doorway, instead forming once more into an undulating blanket; with the drain's churning the water looked an irridescent pink. Not usually prone to tears, Sarah began to cry. Michael punched the door jamb and swore at the tree and even shook his fist at it. Then, for the first time in a long time, Michael put his arm about Sarah's shoulders.

Percy got the note which read,

*Hello, you're cherry trees blossoms are blocking our drains.*
*Please cut it down.*

His eyes watering, Percy's hand shook uncharacteristically as he held out the note to Tom, when Tom came by a couple of days later to take his father to the hospital for more tests. Did people not sign notes these days? demanded Percy in a manner that indicated he thought Tom to be in a position to know.

Tom shrugged. He ignored his father's tone; it must be hard for the independent old man to be so dependent. As a child Tom had followed his father around like a dog: to pick apples, to rugby league matches where he ran out onto the field after his father his pockets full of bandages and Ralgex, even into The Black Bull but, throughout his teenager years their relations soured. Annie used to say that while they could not have been more different physically (where his father was once tall and thin Tom favored his slight-framed mother), the fault lay in them being too—both stubborn, not fond of small-talk, both quick to find fault.

Privately though she observed that Percy resented Tom's having had chances in life, going to college, becoming a secondary school teacher. Chances he had never had. It was this she had spoken of to Tom on her death bed and it was because of this that Tom stuck by his father, even though on occasion he left the house determined never to speak to him again.

"No one's ever complained before, ever, in the fifty-six years I've lived in this house and that tree is as old as I am, when I grew it from a cutting, when I was no but a lad," Percy was saying. Tom blinked, momentarily confused by the unexpected emotions he was feeling. Tom knew his father loved the cherry tree and in a way, for Tom, the tree stood for everything that was good about his father and for what had been good about their times together as a family, one memory out of hundreds suddenly drew clear in his head: Percy in his red striped deckchair in the shade of the cherry tree shelling peas for Annie, with his, Tom's kids, sitting at Percy's feet and eating as many peas as they helped shell. It struck him as unreasonable for someone to want them to take the tree down even if their drain was being blocked. There must be some other remedy.

"Put it out of your mind, Dad." he said. "I'll go round and see if there's anybody to ask."

Tom did go round. But he couldn't see anybody to ask about it and no one answered when he knocked on the doors. Tom told himself he'd go round again the following weekend, but he was so busy marking Year 12 exam papers that he never made it to Percy's. The next few times he did go round to the house on Sandwith, Percy's mind was wandering, seeing buildings out of the window that weren't there. After that Tom did keep an eye out for someone to ask when he was working in the garden, but Tom was getting to the garden rarely these days; he had taken on exam marking in the holidays for a bit of extra money. It was all he could manage to keep taking his father to the hospital, and his wife was beginning to ask questions about how long he could go on with that.

That summer came and went and in the autumn Percy seemed a little better, but his recovery was set back that winter by a fall that broke his hip. When spring came round again he could no longer walk and Tom had to push him in a wheelchair from the car park through the cemetery to place flowers on Annie's grave. Carers were organised to wash and feed him but they did not stop to talk, so Percy spent many hours alone in the house on Sandwith Lane.

When the drain backed up on Blethers for the second time, Percy could not walk out the back to look at his garden unaided, so it was one of the carers, doing the washing up at the kitchen sink that looked out onto the back garden, who first noticed the cherry tree. She mentioned to Percy, as she put her hand on Percy's shoulder and leant in towards his good ear to say goodbye for the day, that someone should have a look at it before it fell over, as it had gone all brown and was leaning to the right.

When Tom let himself in that evening he was surprised not to see his father in the mechanised comfy chair the council had given him. He thought one of the carers must have put him to bed early. He bounced up the stairs, much as he had used to as a child, but his father's bed was made and he was not in it. Worried now, he went back downstairs and through to the kitchen. Percy was not there. Tom called Careline but the man at the end of the phone said Maureen had been in and out at 4pm as expected and had now gone home. She had not left a note to say anything was out of the ordinary.

Tom went through the house again, telling himself everything would be fine, but his father was not in it. He saw the washing up by the sink and as he turned away from it he noticed the back door was ajar. Tom went outside. It was then he saw his father.

Tom ran down the garden. He found his father unconscious but breathing and his face went ragged with relief. Percy's breathing however was shallow and laboured. Tom dialed for an ambulance. Told not to move Percy but to make sure he was warm, Tom found blankets to cover him. It was his father's old crew that arrived, Tom remembered them from the week's work experience he had done, at the ambulance station—was it nearly twenty years ago? "What were you doing out here Percy? It's too cold for a stroll," they said, talking to him continually, gently, as they lifted him into their vehicle. Tom said he would follow in his car.

Percy died later that night. On his way home from the hospital, Tom returned to the garden, to the place where his father had fallen. His father must have crawled to make it this far, Tom thought. Tom stood a while and cried. He wished things could have been better between them. Slowly he walked on down the garden to the cherry tree. The streetlamp had thrown its nearside into deep shadow so that it looked dead. He thought that he was imagining it because of his father but when he went up to it he could see that the tree was listing and that most of the leaves and remaining blossoms were brown. Then he saw the marks on the bark.

Pushing the privet aside, Tom clambered through the fence and examined the other side of the tree. He put his hands out to it, finding the damage as much by touch as by sight. Holes had been drilled down the trunk, the wood pried apart. There were more holes down the side of the tree and nails hammered into the length of the trunk. There was dark staining around the holes, as though the tree had bled. Tom put his nose to the tree and smelled the acrid stench of weedkiller. Whoever had drilled the holes had poured weedkiller into them. Someone had killed the cherry tree.

Tom remembered the note about the drains. He remembered how he had not managed to follow up with the owners of the nearby houses. He felt a heady blackness inside him, a sickness heavy with a sense of failure. Perhaps, if he had done so, his father would still be alive. Tom glanced around. Lights were on in the houses on Blethers. He could go and challenge someone now. Tom lifted his hands from the bark and took a breath and in that moment his knees almost buckled beneath him. He had been up since 5am to get into school early to get an assembly planned. It was past 1am. There was nothing he could do now. He went back up the garden and took the gate that was covered with honeysuckle out to his car.

**About the author:**

Rachel graduated from the University of Cambridge in Social and Political Sciences and then worked in London as a management consultant. Since 2005 she has lived in Cambridge, Massachusetts where she writes for Ben Trovato on fashion film and photography, ghostwrites a blog, and performs interviews with editors and writers for The Review Review. Her interests in work are catholic and include time spent as a kitchen slave, nanny, waitress, cleaner, teacher, secretary, photographer and model.

# COW AND CAT
©2013 by David Empey

The Cow, having tolerated the antics of the stupid cat and its stupider fiddle for as long as was bovinely possible, finally took action. Mooing furiously, she bowled over the obstreperous feline with her horns and ran as fast as she could towards the hillock near the center of the pasture. When she reached the top, she aimed at the Moon, now in its last quarter, and JUMPed.

As she rose high above the farm she mooed down, "Bye-bye, you stupid cat!"

The Cat purred quietly to himself from his perch behind the Cow's right shoulder.

Higher and higher the Cow rose. The farm buildings below dwindled to dollhouses. She saw the neighboring farms spread out to either side, and, far off in the distance, the tall buildings of the city.

"Quite a view, eh?" the Cat mewed.

I wouldn't have thought it possible that a cow could squawk like a chicken, but Our Heroine managed it. "Braawk?"

"Not as easy to get away from Puss as you thought," the Cat continued. Far below, the mountains to the east of the farm came into view. The Earth looked like a giant bowl beneath them.

The Cow finally emitted some nearly coherent sounds. "Who, what, how..."

"How'd I get up here? I jumped up while you were building up speed. You Cows can sure jump but you take your time getting

53

going."

The Cow twisted her head around, to get a good look at the cat. "You...you...you get off! Get off right now! Or...or...."

"Or what?" inquired the Cat, casually. "My, my, that was a close one." A comet whizzed between the Cow's horns.

The Cow bucked furiously but, with no ground to give her hooves purchase, she was unable to do more than wriggle, and the Cat clung easily.

"You can't get rid of me that easily, toots. You may as well accept it—I'm along for the ride. Besides, you're going to need me when we get there."

"Need you?" the Cow scoffed. "Why on Earth would I need you?"

"We're not *on* Earth," said Puss. "And you don't know a thing about the Moon."

"And you do?"

"Certainly."

"What makes you such an expert?"

"I've been there," said the Cat.

The Cow ruminated over this for a minute. Below her, the Earth was a gigantic ball. Clouds hid the outlines of the continents, making it hard to tell if they were over Africa or South America.

"How did you get to the Moon?" she asked.

"That's a long story."

"We've got plenty of time," the Cow pointed out.

"Well, it was like this..."


"That," said the Cow, several hours later, "is the most ridiculous nonsense I've ever heard."

"If you say so."

"I don't believe a word of it."

The Cat shrugged. "Suit yourself.... Say, it looks as if we're going to miss the Moon."

"So, I should hope," said the Cow, ducking her head to dodge another meteor. "You think I want to bang my head on it?"

"But I wanted to go there," the Cat yowled.

"That," said the Cow, "is Not. My. Problem."

"Fine. I'll just have to get there by myself." He clambered over the Cow's head, between her horns and onto her nose.

"Hey, what're you doing? That tickles. Ow! You're pricking by dose!"

The Cat ignored her, and as the Cow rose just above the curve of the Moon and began to sail between its horns, he leapt gracefully from her nose out on to the Moon.

—Or so he intended. In fact, the strap of his fiddle case caught on the Cow's left horn, pulling her over on her head. The desperately scrabbling Cat hooked the Moon with one claw. Cat, fiddle and Cow swung in a graceful half-circle ending with a tremendous THUMP into the side of the Moon.

The Cow scrabbled for a hold with her hooves, the Cat struggled to disentangle his fiddle from her horn. They both used several ungentlecatly and ungentlecowly words, lost their grip, and fell down to the surface.

*WHAM*!

There was silence for half a minute.

The pile of animals, rubble, and musical instruments at the base of the outcropping stirred feebly; pulsated; rolled from side to side. Eventually a hoofed leg extracted itself, then another, another, and another, and the Cow dragged herself out onto the Moon and staggered to her hooves. The Cat dropped neatly to the ground from her head and dusted himself off.

The Cow glared. "Now you've done it!" She stared at their surroundings. They stood at the base of a small outcropping of some soft blue-veined substance. Gently rolling white hills surrounded them on all sides. Off in one direction a tall sharp-peaked mountain jabbed at the sky, and much further off in the opposite direction another similar mountain broke the horizon. She could see no vegetation or water.

'Great. It's the middle of a desert." She took a couple of exploratory steps over the white hills and found them to be unpleasantly springy.

The Cat picked up his fiddle, which had miraculously survived, and cleared his throat. "Not at all."

The Dog stared in astonishment as the Cow charged at the low rise in the middle of the pasture, and chuckled when the Cat leaped onto her shoulder. When the Cow launched herself towards the Moon, he laughed out loud with delight.

"I wouldn't have thought she had it in her," he said to the Dish. "I think she just might make it."

The Spoon surreptitiously goggled at the Dish. "Make it where?" he asked.

"Unless I miss my guess, she's going over the moon, although she might hit it if the Cat weighs her down too much." Turning away from the pasture, the Dog ambled over to the barn and nosed the dog-door open for the Dish and Spoon, who quickly scampered inside. He followed them in and looked around. At the moment the place was deserted, though he could still smell the strong odor of the farm's livestock, the mice, and the rats. He scrambled onto a pile of conveniently placed hay bales and jumped into the hayloft.

The spoon nudged the Dish. "I love this part." The Dish smiled. The dog brushed aside some hay on the floor of the loft, revealing a metal plate set in the wood with a paw-shaped depression in the center. He carefully placed his right front paw in the depression and pushed firmly. A quiet electric hum broke the silence and a mechanical voice said, "Scanning...scanning..." A rubber hose snaked down from the ceiling and began rhythmically sucking in air, for all the world like the sniffing of a gigantic nose. It sniffed the air all around the dog and the two utensils for several seconds, until the voice said, "Identity verified," and the nose withdrew.

"These," the Cat continued, "are the foothills to the east of the town of Selenopolis, where we, or at least *I*, will be—" He broke off suddenly, and continued in an entirely different tone of voice. "What," he almost shouted, "is that?" He pointed at a grayish-blue lump lying near the Cow's left front hoof.

The Cow lowered her head and peered dubiously at the lump. "Beats me," she said. She bent closer and sniffed at it. The Cat was almost dancing in badly suppressed excitement. "Smells like Roquefort."

"What?" demanded the Cat. "Are you sure?"

"Might be Camembert," the cow mused. "Or could it possibly be—" she sniffed again "—Gorgonzola?"

"Yahoo!" yelled the Cat. "We're rich!"

"Rich?"

"It's cheese—*ripe* cheese!" he dashed over to the lump and picked it up.

"*Over-ripe*, to my way of thinking," said the Cow. "I never could understand what was wrong with nice fresh, warm milk, anyway."

"No, no, you don't understand," the Cat meowed excitedly. "Ripe cheese is worth more than gold on the Moon—if we can mine this, we can be millionaires. Now, where did this come from?" He gazed around intently. "I suppose we must have knocked it loose when we smashed into that cliff-side."

"You mean when *I* smashed into the cliff-side," said the Cow, but the Cat had already scampered over to the outcropping, where he jumped up and down.

"It *is*! *It is*! It's a vein of almost pure blue cheese! Stick with me, baby, and we'll go places!" gloated the Cat.

"Fine, whatever," said the Cow. "Look, is there any place around here I can get some grass and water? I'm hungry and thirsty."

"They'll have some in town. Let's just collect some samples…. Now follow me!"

But I'm sorry to have to say that the Cat's schemes, for all their cleverness, proved ultimately futile. His reputation had preceded him and the people of the Moon suspected him, justifiably if not quite correctly, of being up to no good. No one would believe he'd found a vein of ripe cheese; no one was willing to advance him any cheese for a share of the mines' profits; he couldn't persuade anyone to give him even old broken-down mining equipment, no matter how charmingly he purred. It turned out there was a glut of blue cheese on the market. In any case; his cheese mine was suspiciously close to the Royal Lunar Military Testing Grounds; and when he tried to trick—talk—the Mayor of the town into naming the Cow commander of the militia, he and the Cow found themselves imprisoned on charges of attempted fraud, espionage, grand theft horse-and-carriage, subornation of false testimony, aggravated mopery, and felonious jaywalking.

"This is all *your* fault," the Cow complained, and could anyone blame her?

Even so, she found herself assisting the Cat in his foolproof escape attempt, which was most unfortunately foiled by the appearance of the Court Fool at a most inopportune moment.

"And so now I have to drag this stupid thing around," said the Cow, waving a hoof at the enormous ball and chain locked to her left rear leg. "My legs've almost recovered from the jump, too. If it weren't for the weight I could just jump back to Earth."

An insouciant reply trembled on the tip of the Cat's tongue, but catching the look in the Cow's eye, he decided, for once, that discretion might be the better part of valor, and held his peace.

The Cow sighed. "Well," she said, "since I can't jump back, I guess I'll have to try something else. And no, I don't need any suggestions from you," she continued, as the Cat began to speak. "Follow me and do what you're told for once!"

The cat meekly complied as the Cow stalked into the exercise yard of the prison and began stomping her hooves heavily as she walked. The soft cheese gave easily underhoof and she left a visible trail behind her where the subsurface was laid bare.

The puzzled Cat scampered along behind her as the Cow stomped along in a straight line for almost the whole width of the exercise yard, then returned halfway along her previous trail, turned at a right angle, and began a new trail. As she continued, he realized she was creating an enormous letter H, gouged out of the surface of the Moon. His curiosity finally overcame his caution.

"What are you doing? Spelling out H E L P? What good will that do? Who's going to see it?"

"Who do you think?" the Cow replied.

Having satisfied itself, the hose retracted, and with a mechanical hum the loft began to slowly rise, while the roof retracted to show the sky of early twilight.

An opening in the floor appeared and a huge telescope rose up, accompanied by a complicated control panel adorned with dials, knobs, switches, lights, and meters.

Hopping to the eyepiece of the telescope, the Dog began calling out instructions to the Dish and the Spoon, who turned switches and controls at his commands.

"Up a bit more—a bit more—a bit more—down a hair—good—now left—increase compensation speed—STOP."

The Dog nosed a switch, and a monitor on one wall came to life, showing the view through the telescope. The Cow and Cat were plainly visible, rising up towards the moon. "This ought to be good," said the Spoon. The Dog chuckled.

For several days the Dog, the Dish, and the Spoon observed the Cow and Cat at irregular intervals, laughing with glee at the Cat's antics, until one day the Dish noticed something:

"The Cow's asking for help," she said.

"What do you mean?" asked the Dog.

"Look." She motioned to the monitor and the Dog saw the letters H, E, and the beginnings of an L spelled out.

"I see what you mean. I wonder how she knew we'd be watching. Clever old Cow! Well, well. I suppose we should do something."

"Ooh! Ooh! Can we use the Giant Slingshot?" asked the Spoon.

"Oh, you always want to use that," said the Dish.

"But it'll work!" insisted the Spoon.

"The Giant Slingshot," the Dog began repressively, "is *not* an amusement park ride." There was a disappointed-sounding silence from the Spoon. "But in this case," the Dog continued, "I think you may be correct—accidentally. We will use the Giant Slingshot."

"Yippee!" shouted the Spoon. The Dish smiled.

The Dog trotted over to the control panel and deftly manipulated several levers and knobs. In response, the telescope split itself in two halfway along its length, broadening into the shape of a large Y. The two legs of the Y extruded a pair of broad rubber straps.

The Spoon rushed over and buckled the straps together, then seated himself snugly in the hollow of the buckle.

"You'd better go too," the Dog told the Dish. She hopped up next to the Spoon and the Dog strapped them in.

Moving around to the back of the Giant Slingshot, the Dog grabbed with his teeth a leather loop attached to the back of the rubber bands and began backing up to stretch out the rubber.

He closed one eye, took careful aim at the Moon, and released his grip on the slingshot.

"You don't mean the Dog?" the Cat asked.

"No, I mean Sherlock Holmes," the Cow replied. "Of course, the Dog. He's probably been watching us for days with his sooper seekrit telescope."

The Cat was about to reply when he noticed a moving speck of light in the sky. "Look, a meteor."

The Cow looked up. "That'll be the Dog, right on schedule. Get ready!"

And for once, everything went as planned. The Dish and Spoon touched down not two feet from the Cow and Cat, who grasped their hands firmly just before the stretched rubber bands contracted, pulling all four of them quickly back to Earth.

"Great," said the Cow, tugging at the ball and chain. "What am I going to do with this ridiculous thing?"

THE END
...for now

**About the author:**

Dave Empey enjoys role-playing games, science fiction and fantasy, and recreational math puzzles. A computer programmer in his day job, he belongs to 4 Toastmasters public speaking and leadership clubs and 3 informal gaming groups. He's participated in the National Novel Writing Month 4 times and has met the 50,000-word goal 3 times. Someday he hopes to write the Great American Tongue-in-Cheek Fantasy Novel and will get started on that Real Soon Now. First thing tomorrow. Or maybe the day after.

# HELL FOUND ME
## ©2013 by Kathleen Ratcliffe

Hell found me. It found me today in this courtroom. This must be exactly what it is like. Here I am standing in the crowded courtroom; the center of attention. This alone is something I detest. Here I am in a place I never thought I would be, in a situation I still can't conceive. Waiting for the verdict now seems like an eternity passed and is passing again. My ears are burning from deep inside them. The searing continues down my neck. I feel faint and nauseated. A tiny droplet of perspiration travels ever so slowly down the middle of my back. It takes its time as does the reading of this decision. Patience is forced on me. Without choice I continue to wait for the words. Why is this taking so long? Moreover, how did we ever get to this point?

The room looks blurry and out of focus. I look back at my family. Gabriele and Mike are sitting on either side of my mother. While her features are unclear, I can see a hopeful little smile on my daughter's little face. My son's expression is blank; it mirrors that of my mother's. This entire thing has disgraced the two of them. I knew they suffered humiliation on account of the charges against me but was it possible they believed these accusations?

Turning, I see my counsel standing next to me. He, too, has a vacant facial expression. I can't even tell from him what he expects to hear. Time has stopped. All I want to do is learn the verdict. Then I can either begin my sentence or go free. To what? Now that is the question. I am in absolute hell wondering how I will be found: guilty or innocent. Was the hell I lived in for eight long years not enough?

The nightmare started two years ago. I had just ended an extremely grueling shift at work. Exhausted, I sat quietly in the car for a few moments before getting out. The house was abnormally calm. Usually Pete was watching TV with the volume so loud it was amazing that the neighbors didn't complain. One or both of the children would be up which upset me to no end. It did me no good to say anything to my husband. Either he wouldn't hear me because of the noisy television and/or he would ignore me. If he did hear me, all he would do was yell some obscenity at me. Every now and then he would grab me and drag me to the sofa, or, if I was lucky, the bedroom. There he would force himself on me like an animal during mating season. As foul as that was it was actually the best scenario as he would fall fast asleep once he was done.

I hated leaving the kids with that bastard but we needed the money and he certainly wasn't going to work any harder. It was only a few hours that they were in his care—or lack of care. By that time, I had fed them and helped Mike with his homework. There was absolutely nothing Pete had to do but get them to bed at a decent time. I even bathed them before I left, for heaven's sake. But nine times out of ten they would still be up when I came home. They had learned to put themselves to bed when they were tired. Their father never read to them or said prayers with them. He just yelled "get to bed." Nice, huh?

Never in my wildest dreams could I have imagined how things would turn. When I first met Pete, he was charming. He was thoughtful. He was ever so complimentary. He was so attentive to my every need. Not only did he win me over, my entire family was enthralled. Then as suddenly as that wonderful man appeared, he was gone. No, not literally, more like a Jekyll and Hyde thing. I swear he got up to use the restroom on the plane and when he returned, a new, rotten Pete had taken his place. What a demonic persona he had. Did he become possessed by the devil in that rest room? I wonder to this day.

We didn't even have a real honeymoon. We were still on the airplane when he began to flirt openly with every stewardess. He oohed and awed over them. He was demeaning and inconsiderate to me. I was too shocked to react. He hid this side of himself well until it was too late. Once we wed there was no turning back for me. I always believed it was "til death".

I cried that first night as he took me in the most violent of ways. My tears were wasted. The next day I awoke to find I was bruised and sore all over. He never said a word. That's how it was from that point. Instead of signing a marriage license I felt as though I had been sold into slavery. He expected me to be at his beck and call. Pete constantly pointed out other women saying I should be more like them. Flattery was for them now, never for me.

When I announced my pregnancy, he let up a little and was actually nice but nothing like he had been initially. Upon finding out that we had a son he was proud and boastful. But by the time of my second pregnancy he returned to his normal awful self. I was so nauseated all the time during the early months of that pregnancy. Did that stop Pete? Oh no! He was more demanding than ever. If it wasn't for my son I would have picked up and left then. That was hell, feeling so sick, waiting on him hand and foot and having to put up with his tirades.

Things never got better from that time on. Though it was difficult trying to imagine that things could spiral downward from where we were, they absolutely did. But I tried to keep things together for my children. Pete was pretty decent to them most of the time. He was never a disciplinarian. If anything, he was too lax. At least when I was at work I didn't have to worry that he was abusive. Towards the end I began to fear that he didn't watch them at all.

That was my life. Mine and my children's lives, I should say. Not a day went by that I didn't wish I never met Pete. He was a monster who used his size to terrorize. He was the devil and living with him was hell.

I entered the house that night feeling too tired to deal with Pete. Something felt wrong when I came in. It was just an uneasy feeling that I can't explain, though I've had to tell this story over and over. It was just too quiet. The television wasn't blaring. If Pete passed out he'd be snoring loudly. But eerie silence encompassed the dwelling. It was as if the house was vacant and had been so for many years.

Tiptoeing back to the bedrooms I peeked in on my darlings. They were sleeping peacefully, something that doesn't usually happen when I'm not there. At first, I was satisfied to see them at rest, and then an uneasy feeling began to rock my stomach. I started wondering if Pete was even in the house. I had this awful choking feeling when I thought perhaps he left them there alone. He wasn't a great caretaker but at least he would know what to do if there was an emergency. With dread I crept to our bedroom.

The door was slightly ajar but it was dark in the room. I opened it slowly, trying not to make any noise. I could not believe what I saw. There was Pete and a woman sleeping in that bed as if they belonged there. I pulled the door shut and went out to the living room. My head started spinning. The room grew dark. That's when I fainted.

When I woke up I was surprised to find myself on the living room floor. My head was pounding. Looking at the VCR clock I was shocked to see how many hours had passed. Then I recalled my disgusting discovery. What if that woman was still in there with Pete? The thought made me feel queasy. I steadied myself on the lounge chair as I attempted to stand. Slowly I made my way back to the bedroom. The door was wide open. I definitely remember closing it as the shock of the sight overtook my body. The room was still dark and nothing or no one stirred. This time I could see only Pete's massive frame lying in the bed. Where the heck did she go? Inch by inch I closed in on the bed, not wishing to wake my spouse. Unless he was totally passed out, any noise at all would wake him. It was at the foot of the bed that I saw the image that is forever embedded in my brain.

Pete lay there with his mouth gapping open. His eyes bulged as they stared up at the ceiling. Blood was spattered everywhere. I raced to turn on the bedside light. I wanted to scream but managed to cover my mouth with my hands. I did not want the children to see this sight. I kept my hands over my mouth to control the urge to shriek. I was trembling so hard I could barely move. I forced myself to feel for a pulse on Pete's neck. His skin was icy cold. I knew I had to call the police but I wanted to spare the children.

Grabbing the phone, I did what made the most sense at the time: I called my mother. I said there was no time to explain and that I needed to get the kids over there at once. She should meet me at the door, I directed. Then I woke the kids and rushed them to the car. Fortunately, they were too groggy to ask questions until we were almost at Mom's. I mumbled something about Daddy being sick and quickly handed them over to my mother before she could probe for answers about my unusual behavior.

Nothing had changed in the minutes it took to deliver my children to safety. Pete was just as dead as when I left. This was real. It wasn't warm out that night but I was sweating like it was mid-July. Clutching the phone to my chest I took a deep breath before making the call. It was during the drive to my mom's that I realized it was possible I'd be a suspect. But I knew that it would only be temporary. Was I ever wrong!

This past year has been a living hell. I was arrested that night. I spent days answering questions with almost no sleep. I hate going without sleep but I refused to confess to something I didn't do. When they finally took me to my cell I slept for almost an entire day. Strangely it was the best sleep I had in ages.

That cell was later to become my sanctuary. It was there that I could escape the questions, the reporters, the cameras. It was there I could flee from the faces of my family members. They were vocal with support but as each day passed I could see the doubt on their faces. The notoriety of the case was wearing them down.

Every day a new piece of evidence surfaced, making me look worse and worse.

I kept trying to tell the police to find the woman Pete slept with that last night of his life. But all clues led to dead ends. They couldn't find as much as one trace of her in the bed. The entire house was combed for any evidence of her but it was to no avail. Her absence made me look like a liar. I am not.

The coroner had stated that the wounds were made by a smaller adult with average strength. He said they were typical of what a woman would inflict. There were sedatives found in Pete's system, which would explain why he did not fight back. While I have no access to drugs of any kind my lawyer informed me that argument was weak.

The woman must have drugged him, slept with him to throw him off and then stabbed him once she was certain he was unconscious. That is my theory. The prosecution made a similar conclusion but about me. Unbelievable! I wouldn't kill a fly. Why would they presume that I was the murderer? The jury *had* to see my innocence.

My only confession I make right now: that woman, who ever she was, did me a huge favor. I'd never say that to another living soul. Still, she has stolen a year of my life but it is a small price to pay.

My lawyer discouraged me from taking the stand. He came to this decision after reviewing the statements taken during my arrest. He felt that my testimony would be far too incriminating. Yet I knew if I could just get up there and tell my story I would be acquitted. Nonetheless, he refused my pleas.

For years I've had this theory that hell isn't a place with devils and fire. I speculate that it is a place where your worst nightmare keeps happening and re-happening for all of eternity. Another possibility is that one of the worst moments of your life drags out one nanosecond at a time. At this moment I considered that perhaps I was actually dead and this was my own personal hell. What great sin during my life did me in? Surely it wasn't the theft of that chocolate bar when I was in second grade.

I'd never kill Pete or anyone else. I have two beautiful children to consider. How could anyone think I'd do something that would take me away from them? How could anyone who knows me think I would ever bring shame to my children or my family? I have too much to live for. If nothing else, I am a redhead, I look hideous in orange. Ha, hell! You think you found me. Not again. Please not again!

My ears are trying to hear what is being said, but it's as though the judge is mumbling. The speech sounds like a scene in an old movie when the words come out slower than the actor's mouth moves. All at once my vision clears. I can see everything around as plain as day. The foreman is looking up at the judge. The judge is speaking. Suddenly, the speech speeds up to normal rate. This is it. The verdict is about to be read.

The foreman speaks, "We find the defendant...."

**About the author:**

Kathleen Ratcliffe works for a private company as a nurse consultant and instructor for invasive and non-invasive cardiac procedures. She also assists in these procedures in several hospitals in Southeastern Pennsylvania.

She has two children, a son who is a professor of anthropology and a daughter who is a project coordinator for a local medical supply company. Her son also has collaborated with friends to publish a top selling fantasy football guide. Writing is in the family!

Kathleen's husband is also an RN. He works in a nearby hospital in the emergency department. The couple enjoys running, cycling and vacationing in warm climates.

# THE BOOK
©2013 by Karen Dorsey

I've probably walked that beach a million times and never noticed anything there before. But here I am, putting one foot in front of the other, trying to rise above the depression that constantly flutters around my soul. It's not a full-blown horrible I-can't-get-out-of-bed type of depression; it's more like waiting-for-the-next-shoe-to-drop depression. Not really anxiety; I'm not that energetic or focused to grab anxiety. Just a feeling of doom.

It's twilight: the sun is just setting and there are shadows. The crabs are moving around like little gargoyles *snick-snickering* around. It's the end of summer and the beach is more solitary, just like I want it. It wouldn't do for my festering depression to be lifted by happy tourists with laughing children. The wind is blowing a bit—there is always a breeze at the beach, but this has a little chill to it—maybe a warning of things to come.

I've got my favorite outfit on. I've worn the khaki shorts so long the button hangs by a thread and the hem is frayed. There's a stain on the right leg that looks suspiciously like red wine, an astute observation since I gain most of my fruit intake from a bottle. My shirt is fairly new—I bought it for two dollars at a consignment shop—but it's in better condition than my shorts. The deck shoes I purchased over fifteen years ago, but are still in good condition, although I can count on one hand the number of times they've been on the deck of a boat.

I parked my car in the municipal parking lot where, now that the tourists are gone, parking is free. And I don't have to parallel park! I've been driving for years and still can't figure out how to parallel park. Sometimes I'll go out of my way to not have to make a left-hand turn, too.

I'm walking with my head down, discouraging any attempts at conversation in case I meet someone. Being hunched over also keeps sand from blowing in my eyes and allows me to watch where I walk in case a little pile of dog shit finds its way into my path. Folks think they don't have to pick it up if it is just a little dog, but if you step in it, it's still dog shit.

I hum a little song as I walk, something I heard on the radio that is stuck in my head. About five steps ahead of me, something catches my attention. I stop and stare at it for about ten seconds, and then I start looking around, thinking this is a Candid Camera episode. The longer I stand and stare, the quieter the atmosphere becomes and I notice I have almost stopped breathing. Seagulls are circling above my head, waiting to see if I brought snacks, but no human being is in sight. I take a small step towards the thing and stop because it blinked at me. *Blinked*, like light bulb on/light bulb off. *Blink-blink*, then nothing.

I don't want to get too close. What if it explodes or something? I find a stick. A step closer...*poke*...nothing...*poke*...still nothing. Then *blink-blink*...pause...*blink-blink*. With each step closer, another *blink blink*, until I bend down on one knee to get a close-up look. *Blink-blink*. I'm not sure I want to touch it. It looks real, but it's too *surreal* to be real. *Poke*...no response. *Poke* harder...no response. I reach out to grab it and it *blink-blink*s again. Is this a warning? Should I run? No! I'm no coward. I very gently, but firmly, pull it out of the sand. It's amazing! Absolutely the most perfect, incredibly beautiful picture book I've ever seen.

It's not blinking now. I can't even see where the *blink-blink* was coming from. It's perfectly flat and totally closed up, as far as I can tell. How did it get on the beach? Did someone put it there, maybe meaning to hide it? It doesn't seem to have been affected by the sea, sand, or wind. How long has it been here? Why was I the one to find it? Is it a sign? Is it a trick? *Crazy thoughts*, I think. Is this a new mind hiccup I have to deal with? Paranoia? Great, like I don't have enough to keep a lid on.

This thing is so beautiful and clean. I have an overwhelming feeling of ownership. I found it. It's mine. I must be meant to have it, right? If not, the other beach walkers would have seen it before me? Right?

I pull it close to my shirt. Maybe I should put it *under* my shirt. No, I don't like that idea at all—too close to my heart. I make a sudden U-turn and start walking rapidly—but not too fast—to my car with the book pressed to my chest. I will look at it closer when I get home.

I make it to my car, dropping my keys twice before I can focus and get the key into the lock. Now what? I've got to put the book down in order to start the car, but I have a feeling that to loosen my grip will be bad. *Just put it on the other seat*, I think. No, that won't work. Maybe on my lap? No, I have to shift, and it may fall, and that will be *really* bad. I'll sit on it! I'll still have full body contact and no one will be able to see it. I lean over and slide it under my right butt cheek. It is so cold! It wasn't cold when I held it against me.

I am driving home, driving down some of the loveliest streets on the east coast. Of course, I say that, not ever having been to any other street on the east coast, but to me this has to be the most beautiful. The book is hard, but soft and comfortable at the same time. How can that be?

I'm driving home now, feeling like I am in a funnel. The book is hard and soft at the same time. It also alternately burns and chills my butt. Why? Maybe I'm becoming diabetic. Great, in addition to being depressed and paranoid, I'm now a hypochondriac.

I pull into my driveway and lean over to pull the book out. I have to get inside before anyone sees me. Clutching it to my chest, I open the door and Mazie, the dog from next door, starts pawing and jumping on my leg, barking and slobbering. He's supposed to be on a leash in his yard, but he always manages to wiggle out and run rampant through the neighborhood. I usually play and chase him around, throwing a ball—or whatever is handy—and end up giving him a treat.

No play today, though, I have a mission. I have to get inside without anyone seeing my prize. Being forced to share it just doesn't feel right. It's mine, and I don't think the book would like it. Perfect! On top of being depressed, paranoid and a hypochondriac, I'm selfish.

With Mazie now totally frantic because I'm not paying attention to him, I make it to the porch. The front door is my personal nemesis. Being an old house built on part sand, part dirt, and moving and settling, things don't always fit well. The floors are a little sloped, which is easy to live with as long as you're careful where you lay round things. But the doors are an everyday trial. I've been trapped in the bathroom because it was humid and the door swelled shut. I've been confined to the house on particularly rainy days when the doors swell so bad that I can see daylight around three corners but can't get any one of them open. The front door always feels like it is too wide, and when it is humid (almost every day), it takes a strong shoulder push to open it. Better than a burglar alarm.

I slam the door shut, the book again grasped close to my chest. I can feel the *blink-blink, blink-blink*, slow and steady like tiny heartbeats. How can a book have a heartbeat? Is it *my* heart? Do I have heart disease now?

I've got to get a grip. I don't have heart disease. A euphoric feeling comes over me. *Everything's gonna be all right. Have a look. Open the cover.*

I sit crossed-legged on the kitchen floor, in the corner by the pantry, away from the windows, and stare at the cover. It's kind of red—like burgundy, but not so dark—and it shines like those disco pants worn in the eighties. It's hard to describe because when I turn it, the color changes. It's really smooth and feels almost like polished wood, or fabric, or—not. I think I'm losing my sense of touch, but it feels warm against my bare thighs, toes and fingers, like I've just taken off woolen socks and mittens.

Time to take a walk on the wild side. The cover is heavier than I thought, and even though there are no hinges, the book emits a loud rusty-door-on-a-haunted house *kree-eek* when I open it. It doesn't open easy and there doesn't appear to be anything keeping the cover on.

The first page has one black and white photo centered on it, each corner tucked into a black triangle paper-holder. The paper is yellow-gold. It looks old but doesn't feel or smell musty like old paper tends to. There is no sand on the page or under the picture, even though it was half-buried in the sand dune.

I look closely at the picture. The kitchen is dark. I really should turn on the light, but I'm afraid one of the neighbors might stop by, so I make do with the meager sunlight filtering in. I stare hard at the picture, trying to see if I recognize anything. I stare...and the picture starts to move—not the printed picture itself, but the scene in the photo—like a jerky old-time movie.

The photo depicts an old white rowboat resting upside down on the beach with pampas grass growing around it. The grass and sand are moving, as if blowing in the wind. I hear shouting in the picture. How can that be? I see a man running from the right side and past the boat. His shirt is unbuttoned and flaps behind him as he runs. He looks familiar but disappears so fast I can't place him. Another man, barefoot and wearing jeans, follows the first.

The picture has become a video projector—*with sound*!

The view is changing. I feel as if I'm pulling back to get a bigger picture, like looking through a lens, but I am *in* the picture. I can see both men, one chasing the other. I now recognize the man being chased as Clarence Stopper, the president of Eastern US Bank. I've never seen him in anything but a suit and tie, looking very responsible and reserved. Here, he is running barefoot in fairly short-shorts and an unbuttoned shirt, screaming, terrified, at the top of his lungs. Instead of running away, it's as if he's running in place, looking over his shoulder now and then to see if his pursuer is any closer.

Behind him, the barefoot guy in the jeans is running like hell, but not getting nearer. He has a knife in his right hand, holding it as if he's going to stab someone. It's a big knife with a very shiny, almost glossy, blade.

Since the moving picture isn't going anywhere, I can study the full screen. I know that area. It's not *exactly* the same, but it's similar to where I was walking earlier, where I found the book. A few things are different. In the right corner of the picture, I can see an unfinished house I recognize by the staircase. This morning that staircase was just a wood frame. In this picture, the staircase is complete: a beautiful curving double staircase finished with wood railings and stairs. This can't be right, but it *has* to be the same house. I would know if there were any other houses being built with that particular kind of stairway. It *is* the same area I walked this morning, but it's *ahead* of today's time, I try to convince myself.

I glance back at the picture and the action has started up again. Clarence runs back to the boat and crouches behind it. He's bigger than the boat, however, and the other man can see him. Clarence is looking right at me. I swear he can see me as he mouths *Help me* and closes his eyes as the man starts stabbing him in the back.

Clarence doesn't even try to fight. He just stays crouched down behind the boat and takes the stabbing until he finally falls over. The man lifts the boat, pulls it over Clarence's body and starts walking away, stage left. Just before he exits the picture, he turns his head, his eyes focusing directly on me. I *know* he sees me. He gives me a wink and a shy smile, and he's gone.

I sit back against the cabinets, my heart racing—I can hear it in my ears. My breathing is shallow and I feel like I have just run a marathon. My legs are rubbery, my mouth is dry and I am shaking. What just happened?

I look at the book on my lap. The cover is back on and it is again inanimate, cool, and normal. I immediately crawl over to the drawer next to the oven, shove the book in and get up as fast as I can. I run to the bathroom and promptly puke in the toilet, emptying my stomach of the measly amount of crap I had for breakfast and struggle to my feet. I wash my face and swish some water in my mouth. I stagger out of the bathroom and make my wobbly way across the kitchen. I don't even look towards the drawer. Even if it's sending up smoke signals; I'm not touching it again.

When I wake up, it's dark. I must have passed out from too much weirdness. My head aches but not too bad. I stagger into the kitchen and the clock shows nine pm. I must have been out three or four hours. I don't feel too refreshed, though, just extremely thirsty. I open a Diet Coke and lean against the cabinet. I'm trying hard not to look at the drawer that holds the book, but that's exactly where I stare.

Nothing is happening. The drawer isn't glowing green. There's no *blink-blink*. No compulsion on my part to drag the book out. No overwhelming feeling of euphoria. No anxiety. Just confusion and the sense of disbelief at what I saw—at what I *think* I saw: moving pictures in an inanimate object.

What should I do with this picture in my head of Clarence in those stupid short-shorts crouching behind the boat while some guy stabs him? Can I discuss this with anyone? Should I drive by the bank to see if Clarence is working or lying dead under a boat on the beach? Maybe I ought to ask Clarence if he has some short-shorts and if he knows anyone who might dislike him enough to stab him? That's good, I'll just waltz in the bank and lay that on him and see what he says.

I think it's best to ignore the whole thing and pick up some Chinese food from the place on the corner and chalk the whole day up to an overactive imagination. I bet if I look in that drawer, there isn't even a book. I bet it was a bad dream, and I'm worn out by the remnants of that dream still floating through my brain.

A week later the dream is still dancing around in my thoughts. I've tried to forget it. I've not even opened the drawer. Maybe there isn't even a book, maybe it was just one doozy of a dream.

I leave my house with the idea of driving by Eastern US Bank, where Clarence Stopper is president and presumably inside doing bank president stuff. Maybe I'll stop and see if Clarence is where he's supposed to be and not under a boat on the beach. Maybe.

Mazie attacks as I leave the house, and I stop and throw him a Milkbone so he will be distracted long enough for me to make it to the car.

The town never changes. I do love it, though. It's safe and secure and has everything I need to survive. Before I know it, I'm standing in front of the bank. It's an old-fashioned building with big windows and high ceilings, not one of those new pre-fab things. It makes you feel that your money is secure. Most of the employees have been here forever. Some of the women—those with big butts and beehive hairdos—know more about the people in this town than the people themselves.

I stand looking in the window, because I can't think of a good reason to go in. Would spying on the bank president be a good reason? We don't have a great police force, but even one of them would probably find that odd. Suddenly, I'm pushing the door open and going in and I'm not even sure why.

Evelyn Purcelle is the cashier that greets me. Before I can think about it, I ask, "Is Clarence in?"

The look on her face tells it all. "I'm sorry," she says, "he is out today. I'm not really sure of his schedule. Is there anything I can do for you?"

"No," I say. "I'll give him a call later." I almost stumble hurrying out of the bank. Maybe he is just on vacation, or sick, or taking a mental health day.

Maybe he is dead under a boat.

I zombie-walk to my car and sit there a minute to collect my thoughts. No way to get this out of my mind, except to just go and visit the boat.

While I'm driving, I'm considering my options. What if he *is* under the boat? How do I explain how I know that?

I park the car and start walking. The beach is lovely today.

There's a cool breeze and I love to hear the waves. It usually has such a calming effect, but today it doesn't seem to be doing much calming. My heart is beating like crazy. I spy the boat and I walk slower, knowing that I'm probably hunched over because my stomach is growling and I feel nauseous. The boat looks so familiar, just like the movie I saw in my head. I look around, but the sand has covered any footsteps...or blood...or guts...or whatever I expect to see. I look around again to see if anyone is in sight, but I'm alone. I take a deep breath, put both hands under the boat and lift it just a little...

*Oh God*!

When two policemen arrive, I explain that they need to pick up the boat. When they do, they drop it quickly, stumble back and look at each other, then at me. One of them gets on the radio and requests an ambulance and pushes me away from the "crime scene." The other runs to his patrol car for yellow tape to secure the area. My legs are weak and I want to cry.

What seems like hours later, I'm sitting in the back of the patrol car while a different police man drives me home. I have given a formal statement. I said I was following a crab and wanted to see what it was doing under the boat. Everyone bought that story and I was sincerely thanked for my cooperation.

When I get home, I lock the door and pull all the shades. I go to the drawer holding the book. I grasp the drawer handle and it is *hot*! Surprised, I pull my hand back, and then pull down a kitchen towel to grasp the handle. The damn book is blinking again. *Blink-blink. This is too much,* I think as I grab the book. My legs are shaking so bad I just sit down on the kitchen floor in a cross-legged position and pull at the cover. Again, the cover is heavy but appears to be unattached.

The black and white picture is still there, but the boat is gone, only pieces of yellow crime scene tape here and there. The sand where the boat was looks different somehow; nothing I can describe exactly, just different. I stare at the picture but there's no movement to indicate a movie is about to start. It's just a picture of a small bit of beach.

For a minute, maybe two, nothing moves, nothing changes. Nothing but me. I know now that my imagination was totally out of hand that day and I saw nothing unusual in the book. How did I know that the boat hid such a horrible secret? How did I know it was Clarence? I stared longer at the page. Then I see it in the sand about where the boat used to be: something very shiny.

*It's just trash*, I tell myself as I walk towards the spot where the boat used to be. The police had to have searched this area well. No evidence could have been overlooked. Not something as apparent as that big, shiny knife. Yet, as I walk closer, I can see something shiny in the exact place I saw it in the book photo.

I hesitate to disturb it, so I push at it with my foot, scattering the sand rather than bend down to touch it. I don't want to touch it. I don't *dare* touch it! What if it is the murder weapon?

I finally reach down, pull, and of course, it turns out to be a big, shiny knife. I hold it and stare at it. I look around and see a couple walking hand in hand, coming toward me. They are too far away to see what I am doing, so I drop the knife in the sand dune and cover it. *Stay put, you damn thing*, I think.

The couple comes by, say hello and keep on walking. I stand there like I'm frozen. What now? If I tell the cops, they will wonder why I'm back at the murder scene conveniently finding the murder weapon when they had scoured the area earlier. If I don't tell them, and someone else finds it.... It's got my fingerprints on it! Will the sand erase them? I just stand there, staring at the sand, when I hear voices. I turn around and see two men walking this way. They have on sport shirts and slacks and each has a gun; one in a holster around his waist, the other in a shoulder holster. *More cops*, I think. I don't know if our town even has detectives, but I'd bet my first born son that they are detectives.

They close in and recognize me. I guess they saw me at the police station earlier. They introduce themselves as detectives with the county and ask what I'm doing here. What *am* I doing here? Revisiting the site of a murder? Why? Morbid curiosity? Stupidity? I have no answer.

I start to cry. It always works on men, but this time it's for real. I'm afraid I'm losing my mind. The crying starts as a drip and blossoms into full-blown sobs. The detectives look at each other nervously. Murderers they can handle, but with crying women you never know what to expect. I sob, I bend my knees and sink to the sand. What is happening to me?

Later, as I sit on my couch after being carefully deposited home by the detectives, I wonder about the knife. It's still there. I didn't tell them. What if someone else finds it? Who was the guy I saw with the knife?

Out of a wonderful, secure, safe, sound sleep, I'm suddenly awake; sitting up, heart pounding, sweating, anxiety-ridden. I'm afraid with a soul-shaking fear. I sit in my bed, listening. Do I hear anything? Do I *sense* anything? When you live in a house as long as I have, you understand its noises, creaks and groans. I don't hear anything out of the ordinary. What woke me up?

I feel, rather than hear, the book, still in the kitchen drawer, silent and ignored for the last six days. I know exactly how long because I've avoided the kitchen, eating takeout since I was brought home by the detectives. I'm sure my body is now so full of MSG, fat, grease and salt that I have taken ten years off my life. I've had no desire to open the drawer or go anywhere near it. All that time, I thought I was in control. I could decide when and if I gave the book any attention. I'm wrong, because the book is calling me now. Not out loud, but from *inside* me. Inside my head, heart and soul.

I slowly get out of bed, fully expecting an alien hand to reach out and grab my ankle. I tiptoe into the kitchen. I can feel the book blinking. The drawer handle is hot again, so I grab a towel and slowly pull it open. *Blink-blink!* I carefully lift the book and sink to the floor. The book is warm and inviting, but I am less than happy handling it again. I open the cover. Again, a solid creaking sound like the non-existent hinges need oiling. I immediately recognize the picture. It is my street. The view is from my front porch. The street lights are on and the houses are immediately recognizable.

Another moving picture; I can tell by the swaying of branches. A car is approaching, its headlights lighting up the page. I've not blinked for minutes, it seems. The picture gets lighter as the car approaches. I'm not sure how, but I *know* I will recognize the driver.

The car stops in front of my house, and the man who stabbed Clarence turns his head and stares at me. I drop the book, run to the front window and peep through the blinds. It's quiet outside, there's no car out front. Then, the lighting starts to change. A car *is* approaching very slowly.

I can't move away from the window even though I'm terrified. The car stops, and I can see his face as if it's lit with a spotlight. It's the killer! I fall backwards getting away from the window, dropping to the floor and crab-crawling away. I'm practically hyperventilating. I crawl to the kitchen, where I see the picture is back to the safe, beautiful night scene outside my front door.

I don't want to see anymore, and I put the book away in the drawer. I guess it's done with me, because it goes quietly. I stand and realize that crawling around on the floor is not good for anyone my age since my knees hurt like hell and I'm exhausted. I do a shuffle-limp to the couch, lie down, pull the afghan over me and fall asleep.

I wake up, wonder where I am and then see the killer sitting yoga-style on the floor right in front of me.

"Don't be afraid. I'm not here to hurt you," he says.

"That's hard to believe," I reply.

"My actions were necessary," he tells me. "You were called as witness, not participant."

"What does that mean? How the hell did you get in my house?"

"The possessor of The Book has no walls," he says, matter-of-factly.

Somehow, I knew exactly what he meant, and accepted it.

"The eliminated one needed to be stopped," he says. "The possessor is needed to explain."

He is a bit disheveled, his hair needing a trim, but he's not scary or weird looking. He looks at me a long time, then, as if reading my thoughts, says, "The Book decides what form I take. It also decides when to choose a possessor."

"But why *me*?"

"The Book decides."

"What happens now?"

"You will learn to educate and counsel. You will explain why the eliminated one is no longer."

"Counsel? Me? Who do I counsel?"

"The Book will lead you."

I close my eyes and lean my head back against the couch, completely doubting my sanity. When I open my eyes again, it's sunny outside and I'm alone.

Clarence Stopper turned out to be a bad guy. The police ransacked his house and found all kinds of porn, along with several photos of body parts, on his computer. The police and FBI tore up his yard, eventually finding those body parts and other evidence. Later, many townspeople said they felt something was wrong with Clarence, so no one seemed upset that he was gone. I guess it just goes to show that perverts can survive in small towns if they dress—and act—nice.

I never did find anyone to counsel.

The Book has a place of honor in my house. It's wrapped in a silk nightgown and safely stowed in my underwear drawer. I'm waiting for another visit from the midnight guide/banker stabber. I'm hoping I never see him again, but he certainly was cute and my life was almost interesting for a while.

I never look at The Book; I just wait for it to call me, to *blink-blink* for me again. I can feel its energy in my house. I know it will awake again. I can feel it...and I wait.

**About the author:**

At 61, this is my first try at writing fiction and I am thrilled that my story is being considered for publication. I have written other short short stories, and with this bit of attention, I'm sure I will have the motivation to write more! I live in the Charleston, SC area and am blessed to have two great daughters and three wonderful step-daughters with a total of five grandchildren! I can hardly wait to give them my first published story to read!

# NOTES ON TAKING UP SPACE
©2013 by Michelle Wotowiec

On Sunday night Mom cleared her throat, walked down the hallway stairs, and stepped into my bedroom. She said that Uncle Russ was dead and asked me if I was okay. I looked down at *The Mammary Plays* opened in my lap. Page thirty-seven.

Uncle Russ and I were close. He was the first person to tell me that adults weren't always right. He was the first person to teach me how to flip the bird and the only person who taught me how to properly hock a loogie. Last week, while we sat at his dining room table, he asked me if I noticed all of the changes around me. He said things were finally happening and I should pay close attention. Then he gave me his copy of Cormac McCarthy's *The Road*. The very next day I started it at the breakfast table and finished it in the bathtub before bed. I had meant to call him and tell him that I didn't like the way the father talked to the son. I didn't like the dialogue. The distance caused by McCarthy's continued use of "the boy" drove me nuts.

My mother stared at me without relent. She didn't repeat the words *are you okay* but a few tears slipped down her cheek while she waited for my response. I closed *The Mammary Plays* and placed it to my right on the bed. Mom's hair was long and frizzy and her lips were chapped. For the first time, I wondered if she had always looked that way. As a teenager she probably tried harder.

Mom took a few steps back and I saw that she was only wearing one slipper. It was a pink slipper that Dad had gotten her for Christmas. I imagined she was in the process of putting them on when she received the call. With the news, the devastating news, Mom's innate response was to come tell me, not to put on her other slipper.

Two days ago, my sister, Lisa, had just gotten her driver's license and she asked me where I wanted to go. I told her I wanted to play a trick on Uncle Russ, I wanted to cheer him up I said because he was spending his time reading books like *The Road*. She told me that she knew just the place and twenty minutes later we were at The Party Center over on Center Street. They had several different types of whoopee cushions, ranging from one dollar to five dollars. I spent my last five dollars and got the better of the cushions. I hadn't anticipated tax but Lisa helped me out when the time came.

Uncle Russ was supposed to be at Grandma's last night for her sixtieth birthday party, but he wasn't there. The presents, all wrapped in black paper, lined the kitchen counter. No one verbally acknowledged Russ' absence. It was pretty much expected. He rarely came to the family gatherings and when he did he never stayed long. I should have been mad at him for not coming to his own mother's sixtieth birthday party, but I wasn't. When I had decided for sure he wasn't going to show, I stashed the whoopee cushion in the kitchen towel drawer.

Next to my bed, Mom was silent. After I finally nodded in her direction, giving the affirmation that life was going to move on with or without Uncle Russ around, we both made our way to the hallway stairs. She stopped when she reached the window, as if this was something she always did when her brother died, and I ducked past her. I was sure she was looking for him—for his presence. She did stuff like that and I thought it was all bullshit. Besides, I still wasn't sure Russ was dead. I didn't feel his death— in fact I felt the same way that moment as I did any other moment. If Uncle Russ was dead, the world had not changed. That just didn't make sense.

To my surprise, the entire family was upstairs. They had snuck in while Mom and I were having our awkward silence of survival down in my bedroom. There was Dad, Lisa, Aunt Tammy, Aunt Olivia, Aunt Meryl, Uncle Carter, Uncle Steven, and Grandma and Grandpa Crites. The aunts were in the kitchen, elbows on the tile countertop, whispering words like "had it coming" and "it's too bad" and "there was nothing to be done". The two uncles were sitting at the dining room table with Dad, and Grandma and Grandpa sat on the couch, Grandma crying into her sixty-year-old hands. She felt guilty, I knew, guilty for failing as a mother. I watched from the other room as Grandma dealt with a type of sad that I knew nothing about.

Lisa found me right away and took me by my arm. We put on our winter jackets and I followed her out to the porch. We sat on the old swing that Dad's Amish friend had made for him years ago. Lisa told me that she overheard Aunt Meryl tell Aunt Olivia that Uncle Russ did it on purpose. Meryl said that there was just too much heroin to be anything other than suicide. Then Lisa told me that Olivia said that she always thought he would take himself out with a pistol, not heroin. Then Lisa took me back inside and suddenly everyone noticed my existence and huddled around the two of us. The aunts hugged me tight and the uncles rubbed their sisters' backs and everyone was saying what a shame and how life is just too short but all I could hear was the word "purpose".

If I had said anything, I probably would have told them that none of it really mattered—that everything Uncle Russ had said or had been trying to say but couldn't find the words, finally it all made sense. I looked at Aunt Meryl but I saw Uncle Russ. I saw his long brown hair tied back into a ponytail. I saw him bring his hand up to his mouth, his pointer and middle fingernails stained yellow with nicotine. I saw him smile his smile that I always knew wasn't really his. It wasn't his.

Lisa followed me when I walked out of the house, down the sidewalk, and to the car. She unlocked the door before I had the chance to fight the handle. She told me that Uncle Russ was young and I thought that it was weird she used the word *young*. If I was the youngest, and I didn't feel young, then none of us were young. I told her that Russ had told me some things, things that I would never be able to get rid of. Things that I was sure to think about in my dreams fifty years from now, assuming I was still here in fifty years.

I told Lisa that I wanted to go to the market. I was out of cigarettes and the boy at the register would sell them to me. When we got there, Bobby wasn't at the register like he normally was on Sunday nights. Instead, his dad was. Lisa looked at me and grabbed a bottle of Pepsi out of the cooler. I knew she knew that we couldn't just walk in the market and walk out. It would look too suspicious. But to be honest, I really didn't give a shit. Let us be suspicious. Let us be anything than what we were. If Russ was right, and things were changing, we needed to get a grip.

"Is that it for you?" Bobby's dad asked Lisa. I stood behind her and eyed the Snickers, Heath Bars, Hershey Bars, and Butterfingers. Below them were Skittles and M&Ms. Uncle Russ told me once that the authorities did everything on purpose. He told me that even the seemingly haphazard placement of candy bars was planned out. Some big shot guy went to school for a long time and read a lot of studies and came up with the conclusion that a certain placement of colors and shapes was more likely to get my attention than another placement. So, Bobby's dad must have placed these candies in just the right order to get my attention. I heard him tell Lisa how sorry he was to hear the news. He told her that no parent should have to bury their child and I knew he was talking from personal experience. Bobby's little sister was hit by a pickup truck two summers before and the whole town thought the family would disintegrate into nothingness. There were whispers throughout our small country town including the words "where was the father?" and "a six-year-old's body crumbles under a pickup" and "preventable."

Bobby told me once in the basement of the market, while we

smoked the pot uncle Russ had given me, that it wasn't all that hard. He told me that everyone was supposed to feel sad and was supposed to feel helpless and it was all really just programmed and rehashed from things we had heard—things we had been told to feel. He told me that the most innate feeling he had on the subject of his sister's death, the only feeling that he was absolutely sure was his and his alone, was the trouble he had dealing with the empty space she used to take up. It wasn't her he missed, he said. In fact, he didn't miss anything, but instead he found it uncomfortable sitting at the breakfast table with all of this open space to his right where his sister would have normally sat.

I told Lisa when we got back into the car, as I opened up the Butterfinger I had stolen, that uncle Russ was young, but not as young as Bobby's sister. Lisa didn't turn the car on, but looked out the windshield.

"You've got to watch yourself..." she began but I wasn't listening. I thought about Uncle Russ and what space he took up, and then wondered whether or not he was really dead. If he weren't dead, I would tell him that I didn't know a lot about life, but I knew that we only had one and we would find a way that he could make the most of his. He needed to stop reading shit like *The Road*. There is always a way to make the most of it. Then, so he wouldn't think that I went soft on him, I'd say that I had recently been getting the feeling that this is it; when it's over, it's over.

Last Friday had been the first snow of the winter. I walked across three yards and over four fences before I was at Uncle Russ' door. I brought two sleds with me. We weren't all that young, I knew, but everyone likes a good thrill now and then and there was a monstrous hill out back.

I had purposely waited until after lunchtime because everyone knew that Uncle Russ didn't wake up before noon. I knocked on the door but he didn't answer. I knocked harder and still no answer. I looked at my hands covered in the thick white mittens I had used since junior high. There were pink kittens printed on the palms. I took them off. After five minutes had passed and I was sure I'd end up with amputated fingers if he took much longer, I left the sleds on the porch and grabbed a handful of rocks from the driveway. I walked around the house, past the overflowing garbage bins (where I threw the mittens), piles of empty Busch cans, and old car parts, to his bedroom window. The first two rocks missed, but the third one hit. And then the fourth. Finally, I heard him, "What the fuck do you want?"

"It's me!" I said.

"I don't give a fuck who it is—" He was saying as I ran back around the house and to the door.

I waited and he finally came in view, wearing nothing but his underwear. This was the first time I had seen him without clothes on. His torso looked thin and wrinkly, like that of an old man. He had a large marijuana leaf tattooed on his shoulder and a cross displaying a bloody Jesus on his chest. When he saw that it was me his expression changed to a smile and he opened the door.

"Girl, what are you thinking waking me up like that?" He scratched my head with the back of his hand.

The house reeked of smoke and feces. He'd rescued a cat a couple of weeks back, but he didn't know how to take care of it. I saw three spots on the dining room wall where it had sprayed.

"It is almost two in the afternoon. Your ass should be up by now," I said, smiling.

He waved his hand behind him and went into the bedroom to get dressed. I waited in the dining room with the grey and white cat, Kurt. Kurt purred as I scratched the top of his head and below his chin. I picked six fleas from his neck and squished them between my fingernails.

Uncle Russ came back dressed in sweatpants and a sleeveless shirt. He pulled out a pack of Camels and threw one my way.

"Thanks," I said.

"No prob," he said and lit both of our cigarettes.

"How's your mom doing?" he asked, letting smoke slip through his lips. "She still mad at me?"

"She's fine." I couldn't remember why she was mad at him to begin with and I don't think he could either. Everyone was always mad at him, he said. He was just such a fuck up that everyone forgot how to like him.

"Good," he said and grabbed Kurt off the table.

"I think we should go sledding," I said and pointed to the sleds I had left on the porch.

"What are we, five?" he said and I knew he wasn't going to bite.

"You should get out of this house."

"I will when I run out of smokes," he laughed.

In the car Lisa told me that we should go to Russ' house. We should go see what there was to see and maybe it would help me know that he was dead, because she didn't think I really understood. I told her I wasn't retarded and I knew what death was but that I was interested in going to his house. There was something missing, I told her, but it wasn't that I thought he wasn't dead. I wasn't sure what it was but maybe I would find it at his place—maybe it was in the open space.

When we got to his house we saw police sirens and yellow tape. We drove past and ended up at the Denny's about ten minutes north. Denny's was the only twenty-four-hour joint in the area and we decided we would kill some time until everyone called it a night. It was about 9:30 when we sat down and ordered our Pepsis and mozzarella sticks.

"Do you remember when Uncle Russ slugged Dad?" Lisa asked as I lit my cigarette.

"What? No, he didn't."

"Yeah, when Dad had found out that Russ was dealing to a couple of my friends."

"I don't remember that."

"Dad confronted him and told him that he had better shape up. He told Russ he had turned into the biggest loser he ever knew, and that was fine, just as long as he stayed far away from his girls and their friends. You should have seen Russ' face."

"And then what?"

"And then Russ slugged him. Russ said he wasn't a loser and that Dad had sold out. He told Dad that he remembered a time when they were close and Dad wasn't like the rest of them but that time was gone now. But we all saw in Russ' face that he knew different."

Dad and Uncle Russ had been friends growing up. That was how Dad met Mom.

"And then what?"

"And then Dad told him that he was sorry for what he said. He told Russ that he needed help and then just asked him not to sell to my friends anymore."

"Did he?"

"Sell to my friends?"

"Yeah."

"Yeah."

I closed my eyes, "I don't remember any of that," I said.

"You wouldn't. You always loved Uncle Russ."

"Didn't you?" I asked.

"Are you kidding me? The guy was a piece of shit."

I felt my hands begin to sweat, "Don't say that."

"Mags, the guy smokes pot with his teenage niece. He sleeps half the day because he does so much crack that his body can't handle it. He hooked up with one of my friends once, even."

"He did not."

"Susan. He fucked her in his own bed."

I opened my eyes and was suddenly in a world where Uncle Russ was dead and Lisa was telling me nothing but truths. Uncle Russ was dead. Uncle Russ stuck three needles into his arm at once. And then there was the feeling again, that feeling that nothing really mattered.

Bobby came through the door, nodded at the cute blonde waitress and then saw Lisa and me. He came right over and placed his arm around me and told me that he was sorry to hear the news about Russ. Bobby had short dark hair and a muscular build. He had spent a lot of time at the gym over on Liberty ever since his sister died.

"We're going to go to his place in a bit, want to come?" Lisa asked him.

"Yeah, absolutely," Bobby looked over at Lisa but kept his arm around me. I thought about what he had said about space and I thought about the space he was taking. The space I was taking. And then I wondered if we were really doing anything else.

I asked him back when his little sister had died how he had finally come to terms with the open space. He told me that he had made more space. I didn't understand so he explained that he had taken her chair—the chair she sat at during breakfast every morning—to the woodshed and slammed it against the walls. He slammed it until the legs broke in half and then he took an axe and chopped the remains into pieces. When I asked him what he did with the pieces, he told me he burned them. Not all at once, but gradually throughout the winter. He told me they were all gone now, but I had seen one in his dresser drawer only weeks before.

I excused myself and went to the ladies' room. I went into the first stall and sat on the toilet. I read somewhere that the toilets closest to the door are the cleanest. I leaned my head against the wall. That was when the thought occurred to me. I picked my purse up from the floor and pulled out a bag of cocaine that Uncle Russ had given me only days before. He told me not to do it myself. He said pot was one thing and cocaine was another. He told me not to turn out like him. But then he said I could make a lot of money if I sold it. He said it was the real thing—the good stuff—and not to accept anything under a couple grand for it. He told me I could start a college fund and maybe get out of this town.

I stood up and poured the entirety of the bag on the head of the toilet. Then I pulled out a dollar bill and rolled it. I thought about how easy it would be. I remembered something Russ has said years ago: *There is a particular type of sadness that feels good.* I never really understood what he meant. I didn't understand how being sad could feel anything but sad. And I wanted to feel sad—kneeling on the toilet with fate in my hands, I wanted to feel sad. I wanted to miss my uncle. But something was wrong; something about the whole situation didn't sit right with me.

I tried to picture Russ with his needles of heroin. Hadn't I heard that it was three needles at the same time that had finally killed him? Grandma was the one who found him, his face purple and his body covered in feces. I pictured the black rubber band wrapped around his arm, his veins bulging, begging, and I wondered whether he cried. Were his eyes open or closed? I wondered whether what he felt, those very last minutes, was the type of sad that he enjoyed or if it was something different.

I scooped as much of the white powder as I could into my left hand and dropped it into the toilet.

I came back to Lisa and Bobby. Bobby again placed his arm around me and this time I was comforted.

I listened to Lisa tell Bobby stories about our family. She told him that Uncle Russ was the only one out of his five other siblings who didn't have any children. He never graduated high school. He was the family fuck up and yeah, you can blame it on parenting, but the others all turned out all right. Something was wrong with Russ' genes, Lisa told Bobby. There was nothing anyone could do. Bobby didn't agree or disagree with anything Lisa said. Instead he rubbed his hand on my shoulder and said "Oh yeah?" whenever appropriate.

We stayed there in that booth until one am. When we were finally in the car, Bobby asked if I wanted to sit in the backseat with him. I did and he held his arms around me the entire way over to Russ' house. Lisa turned her lights off about a half-mile before the driveway, just to be careful. When we got there the police were gone. Russ' trash was backed up more than I had remembered. I wondered how much was added to the containers since my last visit. The glowing eyes of raccoons looked at us through the bushes behind the bins. I wondered if they knew he was gone. The door was wrapped in a line of yellow police tape and there was a sign reading: *Do Not Cross On Order Of Police*, but we just tore through it.

I pulled out the spare key Russ had given me less than a week before. Right as I was about to turn the key, I froze. "Are you sure you want to do this?" I asked Lisa and Bobby.

Lisa nodded.

Once inside, the house was pitch black. I searched the wall for a light switch.

"What are we doing here?" Bobby asked in the dark.

"We're looking through his house," Lisa said.

"Why?" Bobby asked.

"To see what he was hiding," Lisa said. "There has to be something here that will get Mags to see him for what he was."

I found the light switch. The dining room table was covered in newspapers and an old Cheerios box.

"Let's go into his room," Lisa said.

I had never been in his room. His room was off limits. He told me I wouldn't want to see it and I never questioned him.

Lisa led the way. The police had taped off the bathroom, which was where his body was found.

His door was locked so Bobby kicked it open. I was suddenly back in the world where Russ was alive, and I was afraid he might catch us snooping through his things. He would be so ashamed of me. In his room was a dirty mattress on the floor. There was a yellow sheet balled up and placed at the head of the mattress as a pillow. The small tube television was surrounded by porno videos and three bowls. That was about all of the incriminating evidence to be found: Porn and weed.

Not satisfied, Lisa began to pull his dresser drawers clear to the floor. In them were his underwear, his socks, and about a dozen nicely folded gray tee shirts. She continued searching. In the last drawer she opened were books: Chomsky, Dickens, a collection of poems by Wordsworth, and a few random novels by Steven King.

And then Lisa began to laugh. Bobby squeezed my hand as Lisa turned and faced the wall.

"Who does he think he is?" she said into the sober air.

Bobby let go of my hand and sat next to her on the shaggy orange carpet. We all stayed in the silence until it became unbearable.

"We've got to go," Lisa finally said. "This isn't right."

On our way out, I tried to find the open space that he had once filled, but I couldn't. It was as though he was never there at all.

Lisa pulled into Bobby's driveway. The car was parked and I waited for him to get out. Instead he pulled me toward him and kissed me. We had kissed before, several times, but it was never like that. The stoned and drunken kisses were nothing more than our bodies connecting. Bobby looked at me and told me that he was there if I needed him and I knew he meant it. We were growing older and we were finally doing it the right way, I thought. And then he left the car, closed the door, and snuck into his bedroom window.

"He has had a thing for you for years, Mags," Lisa said as she pulled the car onto the street. I stayed in the backseat.

We slipped into the house undetected. No one had even noticed we were gone. Our presence wasn't important when compared to Uncle Russ' departure. I was sure that while we were away, the aunts and uncles and grandparents all cried on one another's shoulders. When they were done crying, they probably tried to recall some good stories about Russ. Maybe they told the story about how when he was only nine years old he won a countywide essay contest on how to make the world a better place. Grandma would describe the picture in the paper: Uncle Russ holding his award in one hand and his other hand held high in the air. He wore a real smile in that picture. And then they probably cried some more when she was unable to recall what the essay actually said.

Everyone was sleeping in the living room. The aunts were

sprawled out across the two leather couches and the uncles slept on the floor. The cousins, who must have shown up while we were gone, had brought five cots and set up camp right there in the living room with the rest of them. Mom and Dad slept entangled like a pretzel and to their right was Grandpa holding Grandma tighter than I had ever seen him do before. Everyone was sleeping in the mix and something about the whole ordeal felt real. Despite that feeing, I had this terrible feeling that maybe it was all just too late. Maybe this random fight for survival was already lost. I didn't say this aloud, but instead followed Lisa and together we took up whatever space was left in the room.

**About the author:**

Michelle Wotowiec is a twenty-six-year-old Cleveland woman who holds an English MA and loves cats. Her hobbies include practicing a vegetarian diet, bicycling, traveling, watching movies, and reading contemporary realistic fiction. She also serves tables full time because she loves people and she loves the money.

Michelle focuses on appreciating the people and things around her for their own unique qualities. She has pretty much decided that happiness is really what it's all about. Writing makes her happy.

She spends her free time editing and maintaining The Watercress Journal. She is currently in the process of deciding where to go from here.

In her own writing, Michelle strives to write relatable and timeless pieces that leave the reader feeling fulfilled.